Book Two in the
Ties that Bind Series

Libby

FAY
LAMB

Libby

© 2014 Fay Lamb

ISBN-13: 978-1-938092-62-6
ISBN-10: 1938092627

This book is a work of fiction. Names, characters, places, and incidents are either products of the author's imagination or used fictitiously. Any similarity to actual people and/or events is purely coincidental.

Published by Pix-N-Pens, 130 Prominence Point Pkwy. #130-330, Canton, GA 30114.

www.PixNPens.com

Printed in the United States of America.

Lovingly dedicated to the memory of my grandmother,
Elizabeth Fay Thompson,
who never failed to let me know by word and by deed how
much she loved me.

Chapter One

Libby Overstreet's gaze remained fixed on the front door of Java Lava even after her friend, Charisse Tabor, arrived for their morning ritual.

He had to arrive soon or her entire day would be ruined.

The assortment of usual customers entered the shop. Some remained, sitting in brightly colored chairs surrounding mocha colored tables. Others took their coffee and donuts, bagels, scones, and other delectable morning treats with them.

Libby leaned forward, cupping her chin with her hand. Where was he?

"Hey." Charisse waved her hand in front of Libby's face. "Good morning."

"Morning." Libby smiled and sipped her caramel-flavored iced coffee. She had good news to tell her friend, but distracted beyond measure, she could do nothing but wait.

"I try to get here a little earlier every day, but you always manage to arrive before me." Charisse pulled out a chair and sat. "I should warn you. My big lumbering bear is meeting us here this morning."

"Uh-huh." Libby returned her gaze to the door. Looking at her watch, she let her shoulders slump.

"Are you expecting someone, too?" Charisse turned toward the door and then back to Libby, her eyebrows arched.

Libby flushed with warmth. Her cheeks probably looked on fire. She'd never told her best friend about her object of desire. "Not really. Delilah said she might join us." She'd never lie, not outright, but she wouldn't want Charisse or Delilah James to laugh at her foolish heart.

"Oh, great. Two not-so-morning people. I don't know which one is worse, Gideon or Delilah." As she did every morning, Charisse turned her attention to the counter and the goodies in the glass case. She rubbed her hands together, her gaze fixed on the treats just out of her reach. "I think I'm going to have an éclair. Want one? There are only three left."

The enticing scent of baked goods mixed with the undeniably rich aroma of coffee held sway over Libby daily. Today, as usual, though, she shook her head.

The door to the coffee shop opened. Libby sat straighter. She ran a quick hand through her hair, and drank up the sight before her. As far as she was concerned, God had broken the mold with this man. Neatly trimmed brown hair touched the collar of his soft blue shirt, bangs brushed to the side. His eyes, the color of rich maple syrup, shined when he smiled, and when he was tired those same eyes reminded her of a sweet puppy that only wanted to curl up and find rest. And my goodness, she'd seen him laugh once, and she'd gotten lost in the sound of it, and in the way the laughter reached those gorgeous eyes. Sometimes, like today, he shaved;

other times, he wore a shadow of a beard. Either way, when he walked through that door every weekday morning, Libby had to remind herself to breathe.

But that was only the outside. She had no idea about this man's heart—if he was gentle. If he loved God.

Still, he was such a sight to behold.

Now, if she could only keep from staring.

"If I don't get two of those éclairs, I won't have anything to coax Gideon into a better mood." Charisse sprang from her seat and stepped into line.

Libby couldn't look away from the man. She first noticed him among the crowd of coffee drinkers a month before. As the days passed, she realized it was his habit to frequent the shop each morning. A creature of habit, he arrived around the same time. Could he have been here all along, and she hadn't noticed him before she'd taken up her new career as a stalker?

He sat in his usual chair and laid down his newspaper. Then he raked his fingers through his oh-so thick hair. He looked in her direction and that gorgeous smile lit his face.

Libby lowered her head, turning her cup of iced coffee around as if she'd found something of interest there. She thought of taking a sip, but she couldn't do it naturally enough to keep from looking like a fool.

"There. Got 'em." Charisse returned with a tray filled with two coffees and her two éclairs. "Gideon can go to his courtroom a happy man. I don't know why he's complaining. He's the one who called the attorneys in at seven thirty this morning. He stayed up late praying about his ruling."

Gideon entered the shop. He looked nothing like the lumbering bear Charisse had described and everything like the genial, sweet fellow Libby had known since high school. He didn't move directly toward his wife. Instead, he veered in the direction of—goodness—did he know her mystery man?

"Evan Carter," Gideon's voice boomed as he shook hands with the object of Libby's unwavering attention.

Evan Carter.

She would never forget that name.

And Gideon knew him.

Gideon waved in their direction, and Charisse held up his éclair. He winked at his wife, waved to Libby, and turned his attention back to his friend.

"Evan's here every time we are. Imagine that," Charisse said.

Libby's gaze remained fixed on Gideon's handsome friend.

"But you've been doing more than imagining. You've been waiting for him to walk in." Charisse lowered her voice to a conspirator's tone.

Libby wouldn't acknowledge Charisse's accusations. If she did, she'd only dig herself into a deeper hole.

What was it about this man that drove her to distraction? She knew nothing about him, yet she thought of him throughout the day and at night—oh, goodness, every night. She could barely say a prayer without his handsome face entering her mind. Then she'd done something she'd never dared do before. She'd prayed God would give her this man to honor, protect, and love her—no, not love.

Cherish.

"Libby?" Charisse leaned over the table like a teenager telling a secret. "I'm right, aren't I?"

Libby took a long sip of her drink. Instant brain freeze. Now, look what Charisse had done with her interrogation. Libby pinched her eyes closed trying to quell the pain in her temple. When she opened them, Charisse was no longer sitting at the table. She stood at Evan's table talking with the two men.

If Charisse dared to embarrass her, Libby would never forgive her.

"Glad to see you again, Evan. Have a great day." Charisse waved and stepped back to the table. "Sorry about that," she apologized.

Libby let out the breath she'd been holding and nodded. Then Gideon and Evan both stood, and she gasped.

Charisse gave her a sharp look and then smiled.

Had Charisse meddled? She and Gideon were always trying to match her with someone. Hadn't they learned there wasn't a man on the face of the earth who'd find her desirable? What did she have to offer? Her entire life had been spent taking care of her ailing mother until her mother's death earlier in the year.

Evan left his newspaper on the table. Obviously, he didn't plan on sitting with them. Why would he? One good look at her, and he no doubt would run in the opposite direction.

"Libby Overstreet, I'd like you to meet a friend of mine, Evan Carter," Gideon introduced.

Libby pushed her glasses up on her nose. "Hi, Evan."

"Good to meet you," he said and held out his hand. "Gideon told me you're thinking of buying the old Nardone's Nursery."

Libby nodded. She did her best to keep the tremors from her hand as she slipped hers into his. His fingers gently enveloped hers in the softest of touches. Her imagination ran wild, pretending Evan held to her for a second or two longer than required and that he seemed hesitant to release her.

When he did pull away, she put her hands into her lap and lowered her head.

"I know the place," Evan said, and Libby looked up. She could almost convince herself that the warmth wasn't always there in his eyes, and that his smile was just for her.

"Libby?" Charisse nudged.

"What? Oh yes." She shook her head to clear her thoughts. She hadn't told Charisse or Gideon the steps she'd taken to secure her dreams. Now she had to tell them in front of a stranger—an extremely attractive one at that.

"I put an offer on the place yesterday." She forced her gaze from Evan to Gideon. "They accepted all the contingencies you told me to add, Gid. I have a week to get the place inspected."

"You put in a threshold for repairs?" Gideon asked.

"They have to pay for any repairs over a certain amount or forfeit the contract and return my escrow."

"And that's where my buddy Evan comes in. Perfect timing running into him today." Gideon clasped his hand to Evan's shoulder and glanced at Charisse.

An all too familiar silent conversation took place between her friends. Without a doubt, they were up to something.

"I don't understand." Libby swallowed so hard Evan probably heard her gulp.

"Among his many talents, Evan's an architect and a contractor. I call him an over-qualified builder." Gideon elbowed his friend.

"Can I help you out?" Evan's brown-eyed gaze seemed sincere enough.

"I don't have the money to pay an over-qualified builder—I mean—an architect." But if she did, she'd give him everything she owned if it meant they could work together on the project.

Evan smiled. "I sometimes barter jobs, and I'll even take the risk. Let me inspect the place for you, and if everything works out and you make the purchase, I'll trade some shrubbery for a personal job I'm working on."

"But even I know the place is rundown. What will I do for you if I can't purchase it?"

"Like I said, I'll take the risk." Evan's smile leapt into her heart and took ownership.

"Nope," Gideon said. "Libby will cook you dinner

for a month."

"Gideon Tabor." Charisse gave him a playful slap.

Good. She needed to admonish her husband.

"That's a great idea." Charisse turned a mischievous smile in Libby's direction.

Treason. Her friends had betrayed her. But in a nice way, she had to admit.

"So, what about it? Is it a deal?" Evan held out his hand once again.

Libby reached across the table. His hand was warm in hers, reaching into emotions she'd closed off long ago. In his gaze, though, she could almost swear she saw admiration. Men never looked at her in that way. They looked beyond her, never saw her, and this one—the one who'd caught her imagination on file—was being so nice.

With a nod of her head, her tears flowed.

Evan pretended to read his paper. He'd excused himself and returned to his table when the woman started to cry. Why her emotions overcame her, he couldn't say, but those teary green eyes endeared her to him even more.

Libby Overstreet.

Now, he knew her name.

For several weeks now, Evan had struggled with approaching Charisse Tabor. He knew her through church and as Gideon's wife, but his actions would have been insincere since he really only wanted to meet her friend.

At night, he played out the scenario in his mind. "Hi,

Charisse. How are you? Do you remember me? I'm the guy who had to stand in front of your husband, the judge, on a DUI? I'd love to meet your gorgeous friend. Do you think she'd be interested in a recovering alcoholic with a mean temper, and hideous scars covering his back?"

Yeah, he just wouldn't go there, but he had prayed. He'd promised the Lord that he would never treat a woman with disrespect again. If God had someone for Evan Carter, He would open the door.

But from his first sight of Libby, Evan felt as if God was whispering, "This is the girl. She's the one I have for you." Still, he'd prayed for that open door, and God sent Gideon.

And Gideon took it upon himself to introduce Evan to the woman of his dreams.

Libby.

A beautiful name for a gorgeous woman.

"Evan?"

He turned toward the familiar voice and stood. "Delilah, good to see you." Delilah James was not only a friend from his past. She was a friend and colleague of Gideon's. Evan had been surprised to find she attended the church Gideon had invited him to visit—the church where he'd met and began a relationship with Christ. Delilah was also friends with Evan's ex-girlfriend and the current tormenter of his life: Hope Astor.

And someone had said that Orlando was no longer a small town. He'd beg to differ. Sometimes, the city wasn't large enough.

"Evan, I'm so glad to see you." As if summoned, Hope's light touch fell upon his arm. "Christa's throwing a party, and I promised you'd come. We can have dinner and show up a little late."

Evan rubbed his forehead where the throbbing began to beat a steady tempo. Yeah, the place was so tiny he couldn't escape these little chance meetings if he tried.

Delilah wiggled her fingers in good-bye, leaving him alone to face Hope. Evan wished he could join Delilah at the other table and get to know Libby a little better. He'd only stepped away because her tears seemed to have embarrassed her. He didn't want to add to any burden she carried.

Now, he had to face his most difficult challenge, the clash of past versus present.

"So are we on?" Hope asked.

He took a deep breath and released it. "Why'd you make a promise without asking me first, Hope?"

"Because I know this little phase of yours can't last much longer. You need to get out and party. Let yourself go."

Ah, the past, always calling to him, "Come out and play. You can do it. There's nothing wrong with enjoying your friends and having a good time." But the last time he'd given in, he had not enjoyed the company of old friends. God had given him a glimpse into what he must have looked like to others not so long ago. Not a good picture.

"You never go anywhere. You're such a bore," Hope taunted.

His buddies who attended the weekly meetings, his church's equivalent to Alcoholics Anonymous, didn't think him boring. They liked him. Said he was a born encourager. He only wished he could believe them.

"I have plans this evening." He didn't ask her to sit, but she sat anyway. He preferred to remain standing. "What about Daniel Duvall? Is he still playing hard to get?"

Even he had to admit that sounded harsh, but Hope wasn't an easy one to put off.

Hope's lips made a perfect straight line and then she shrugged. "Danny's too busy for me."

Even in the days when Evan thought he had something going with Hope—something very inappropriate—anyone could see that she only used Evan as a diversion. Her dreams revolved around Dr. Duvall, and for some reason, Danny Boy wasn't taking the bait. "Well, as I said, I have plans myself."

"Oh, really? What are you doing?"

"Work." That wasn't a lie. Gideon and Libby were meeting him at the nursery this evening for an inspection. What did it matter if he looked forward to the job or to seeing Libby Overstreet again?

"Well, after work, join us at Christa's place. She always throws such a bash."

Yes, she did. His old clique didn't consider a party a *bash* unless the cops were called out at least three times. What fun was a party unless you could mock the men hired to protect the city from people too drunk to know they shouldn't be behind the wheel of a car?

He'd driven like that one too many times. Wasting law enforcement resources that would better be spent elsewhere. He'd meant the last such trip to be the end for him. Turned out God had plans. Despite his best effort, he'd survived the crash, and Evan hadn't driven drunk since—hadn't taken a drop of liquor or swallowed one bit of illegal substance.

"You're up early." He looked at his watch. "Did you get a job?"

"Artists can work any time, Evan. Actually, I just left a party. I'm on my way home to rest up and get ready for Christa's."

As if a headache wasn't enough, Evan rubbed the back of his neck where tension was building. If Hope wasn't careful, she would wake up one day and find that while she danced her nights away, life was passing her by. With his head lowered, he dared a peek at the sweet brunette at the other table. Libby's eyes met his.

He smiled at her. Libby's lips turned up a bit before she looked away.

Hope followed his gaze. "Poor girl. Someone needs to show her how to wear her hair and get her a new pair of glasses. A new wardrobe and a touch of makeup wouldn't hurt her either."

Evan kicked the chair in front of him, scooting it under the table. "Gotta go."

"Can't you stay?" Hope whined.

"No. I have a busy day, and I need to find time to stop and see Nate at the nursing home."

"Why? You finally got rid of the old coot. He treated you horribly. I've seen what he did to you."

Yes. To his shame, Hope had seen Nate's handiwork. "He's my father, and I have the same responsibility toward him I had with my mother."

He tried not to look in Libby's direction, but when he did, he caught her staring at him. And again, she lowered her gaze.

Today, God had allowed him to meet the sweet young woman he'd been watching for weeks, and Charisse had said Libby wanted to meet him. He'd almost forgotten his past and what the future could be for any woman who got too close to him.

"Evan?" his past called out to him again.

Hope had seen him at his worst. She seemed to delight in the person he used to be: that sick, soulless creature, who always wanted to fill his heart with drugs and alcohol so that he could feel something—most often anger that when stoked just right would turn into rage.

He couldn't go there; he wouldn't go there.

"I'll see you around, Hope." He walked out the door.

Chapter Two

Libby signed in at the front desk of the Crystal Lakes Health and Rehab Center. She waved to the volunteer standing at the copy machine before moving into the main reception area and down the hall.

Pictures of seascapes hung at regular intervals on pastel green walls. White wicker furniture sat in the visiting areas, their muted cushions of pink, white, and sky blue all blended well with the decor.

Libby stopped in the doorway of one of the two recreation centers. Scarlet Trevetti sat alone in her wheelchair.

"Libby, girl, you look beautiful." The older woman beamed and held out her hand. "Have you found a husband yet?" She winked.

Libby shook her head and pushed a smile into place. Scarlet asked her the same question every time Libby visited with her, something Libby did frequently since moving to Orlando after her mother's death. Her mother had ministered to the elderly, and Libby felt at home with them. The discarded seniors, those who never received visitors or communication from the outside, were the ones God had placed upon Libby's heart.

"Oh, well, honey, you aren't going to find him here. They're all too old. I won't even look at them." Scarlet cackled at her own joke.

Libby laughed, her mood lightened. "You need to behave," she chastised her older friend.

A woman dressed in scrubs walked past the door and then backed up. "Mrs. Trevetti, I've been looking all over for you. Time for your physical therapy."

Scarlet rolled her eyes at the young therapist.

Libby moved aside to allow the therapist to wheel Scarlet away. She'd prayed for the opportunity to again broach the subject of Scarlet's relationship with the Lord. Apparently, today was not the day.

She walked down the hall. Her plan was to first introduce herself to some of the newer residents and make a friend or two. Then she'd stop in and see others she hadn't visited for a while. She reached into her purse and brought out a handful of the gifts she'd made for the occasion and stopped in front of Room 225.

"Nate *Carter*," she whispered the name.

Plenty of Carters in the world, but none of them as handsome as Evan.

And she'd be seeing him again soon. She didn't have to wait to see him at the bakery in the morning. She stopped for a second at the memory of Evan's hand in hers. His touch had stolen her breath away.

She'd better dream while she could. In a few hours, the thrill would be replaced by the truth. She'd have more of a chance with the elderly Nate Carter than she would with the handsome young man who'd captured her imagination.

She knocked and then pushed open the heavy door.

"What do you want?" The older man sat in bed, a tray of food in front of him, his hands balled into tight fists.

Libby stepped closer. "Hello, Mr. Carter. My name's Libby Overstreet. I wanted to bring you a gift and see how you're doing this afternoon?"

His thick white hair was mussed. Emptiness replaced a momentary flicker of life as if he'd left her for another day and time, not connecting with this world at all.

Libby held out her small present, a tatted bookmark made from a cross pattern she'd created then stitched in green thread.

The man reached for it, unclasping his fists to yank it from her hand. He studied it before giving her his attention. "I'm not going to church today." He lowered his head and then raised his chin, reminding Libby of a defiant child.

Libby smiled. "You don't have to go today. The Lord can meet you here."

When Mr. Carter looked away, she turned to leave.

"You'll come back, young lady, won't you?" For all his gruffness, Libby recognized the desire for companionship.

She nodded. "Yes, sir, I'd love to visit again. God bless you." She backed out the door, closing it with a soft click. "Dear Lord, please wrap Mr. Carter in your loving embrace today," she said the prayer, turned, and bounced off a warm body.

"Whoa." Strong arms reached out to protect her from

falling.

She glanced up into familiar brown eyes that remained vivid in her memory most of the day. Now, if possible, they offered her even more tenderness than she'd seen earlier that morning.

"Libby," Evan said.

The tone of his voice seeped into the very center of her being. He remembered her.

"Evan, I'm sorry. I didn't see you standing there."

"Funny to bump into you here," he teased.

She suppressed a giggle. Such girlish behavior would surely make him run in the opposite direction.

"Are you visiting someone?" he asked.

She held out her bundle of crosses and handed him one. "I like to give gifts to the residents."

He turned the lace work over in his hand. "Did you make this?"

She nodded. He really seemed interested, but she was sure he was only acting nicer than most men would normally do around her.

"Intricate. I like the design. How'd you learn?"

"My mother taught me." Wow. He really did like it.

He continued to look at the cross, which was made of double knots and picots—a simple tatted design. "I've never seen anything like this." Finally, he gave her his attention.

She managed to keep eye contact, but her face burned. Any second now and she'd break out in an unladylike sweat. "Thank you."

"Thank you." He held up his gift. "I'll use this in my Bible."

He read his Bible. Could the man get any more desirable?

"I better go in and see my dad." Evan nodded toward the room behind her.

"Nate's your dad?"

He closed his eyes and nodded before speaking. "Yeah. You gave him one of these?"

"Of course."

He opened his eyes. "Libby, was he nice? He didn't threaten you?"

"No, he was very sweet. He asked me to come back." She touched his arm.

His body tensed, and his gaze fell upon her hand. Did he not like to be touched—or did he not like her touching him? She pulled away.

"You might not want to visit him." He continued to look at his arm where her fingers had been moments before.

"I—I didn't know he was your dad."

"He can get violent. Anything can set him off. I wouldn't want him to harm you."

"I did promise him I'd come back." She shifted her weight. What was the appropriate protocol in this situation? Should she leave or say something else?

"Be careful, okay?" He held her in place with a steadfast gaze.

"Evan, I'm sorry. This can't be easy. Do you have

family to help?"

"He ran my brothers off long ago. I'm all he has left. I tried keeping him at my place, but he's strong. His rage terrified the home healthcare nurses, so that's why I moved him here."

"Well, I'll let you visit with him." She shouldn't act too needy. Move on.

"I'll see you in a bit anyway."

"Yes." Libby placed her hand over her heart, afraid Evan would see it pounding against her chest. "I'll see you at the nursery." She walked down the corridor. At the corner, she leaned to peer back down the hall. Evan was still watching her. Once out of sight, she heaved a sigh. Evan Carter was as wonderful as she'd dreamed, and he'd talked to her.

A girl could only hope.

"Let me see what color I want this week." An elderly woman in a wheelchair reached up with her gnarled hands.

"Mary, how are you today?" Libby leaned down, thankful for the distraction.

Evan looked again at the rich deep red of the cross Libby had given to him. How could a hastily said prayer and a small gift both convict his soul and tell him so much about the giver?

Had he remembered to pray for Nate this morning? He hadn't actually forgotten to pray. He'd stubbornly refused, letting bitterness churn within him. Libby's sweet, spoken prayer convicted him.

"What Libby said, Lord," he whispered and stared at the bookmark.

Red was the color he thought of when he imagined God's forgiveness. When he looked at Libby, he envisioned newness, like that given to him because of Christ's sacrifice.

Forgiven, yes, but a new beginning with such a sweet woman? For him? He'd dared to dream, but he didn't believe so. God would soon close the door. The Lord would not put such a precious heart in Evan's destructive path.

Evan's artistic eye followed the knotted thread. Libby had started at a central point and worked her way around to complete the cross at the same place where it had begun. The knots reinforced the strength. Evan knew so little about her, yet, despite her earlier tears, a peaceful strength radiated from Libby Overstreet. Christ was her core, and like the pattern in the cross she'd made, everything about her started and ended at the Center.

If Evan wasn't careful, he'd almost believe Libby's friendship could help him overcome all his obstacles. He needed to take care. His burdens belonged to God, not that sweet woman who'd probably fall under the load.

He pushed open the door to the room and peered inside. Satisfied there would be no immediate confrontation, he entered. His father didn't acknowledge his presence, and Evan pulled up a chair and sat.

Nate turned, and Evan fought to stay seated. "How are you doing today?"

"They never give you enough to eat in these military hospitals. I'm starving," Nate glared at him.

"The old wound's kicking up again, huh?"

"Yeah, it is. Did you see the pretty nurse? She just left here." Nate held up his own gifted cross.

"She is pretty, isn't she?" Evan relaxed and smiled. "Her name is Libby. You should be nice to her."

"I'm always nice." Nate slammed his hand down on the table. His tray clamored, but the food remained intact in front of him.

Evan jolted from his seat. "Yes, sir." The words flew from his lips. Would he ever get over the fear Nate instilled in him? His father was nothing more than a frail old man. Evan didn't understand how he could be so strong when the rage took control. And Nate's one controlling emotion was fury. But Evan's apprehension ran deeper than the physical. What scared him most were the psychological scars his father had left upon him. His cowardice as a child and even into his teen years made Evan search for solace and a way to diminish the fear. He's found it with alcohol and drugs.

More than once, Evan had flown into an alcohol-induced wrath. In his sobriety, could he trust himself to love someone so much he wouldn't let his guard down and, in anger, harm them?

"Admit it, boy. I'm always nice," Nate demanded.

"Yes, sir, you are."

Nate turned his steely gaze to Evan. Evan's

submissive words must have stirred something in Nate's memory. "Your momma was nothing but a tramp."

Evan lowered his head. Sometimes that worked to appease the old man, but no matter how much fear Nate instilled in him, Evan would never disparage his mother. Denise Carter had done her best to cope the only way she knew how—with denial.

After a long while, he raised his chin. Nate again stared off into nothingness, ignoring his presence. Evan slinked to the door. In the hall, he leaned against the wall and pressed his hand over his eyes. He would not allow Nate to evoke emotion. His mother didn't need defending any longer. Nate's words couldn't hurt her now. Why, then, did they pierce Evan's heart like a poison-tipped spear, causing the bitterness to spread through his veins?

The murmur of elderly residents talking to no one in particular frayed Evan's last nerve. The *clip-clop* of a walker sounded as someone tottered down the hall. Evan took a deep breath and rued the action. The smell of the day's dinner mixed with the stagnant odor of impending death.

The stench was not new to him, and his father had reminded him of it. The woman Nate called a tramp had waited on Nate hand and foot, sometimes with broken bones and swollen eyes. She fed Evan's father his meals despite the fact that with a broken jaw or swollen lips, she couldn't eat at all.

Then when Evan and his brothers were grown, she left Nate and his beatings behind. In her last days, she had returned to Evan, and he'd become her caregiver until her death. He'd barely recovered from his grief when the authorities told him about Nate's midnight rants, his brandishing of guns, his threats to kill neighborhood children. At first, Evan told them to make the world a safer place and take Nate to jail. They had, and three days later a social worker had stopped by Evan's office. The mental exams leaned heavily toward Alzheimer's.

As part of his sobriety, Evan had promised never to shrug off a duty, and he determined to provide his father the best care. If he didn't, it would be only a matter of time before Nate, in his deteriorating mental state, killed someone. Only by God's grace had his sons and wife survived the torment Nate had put them through.

And even with the best care money could buy, Nate didn't make it easy for him.

Evan slammed his fist backward. It hit the wall with a loud thud.

"Oh." Libby apparently saw his outburst of emotion.

Evan straightened but kept his eyes shut. He didn't want to see the fear on her face. Instead, he ran his hand over the tatted cross in his other hand.

"Evan?" Her concerned tone dissolved the venom of bitterness.

He forced himself to look at her. Green eyes filled with sympathy, not fear, returned his gaze. She offered him a smile that flitted away as quickly as it came.

He raised his hands in surrender. "I'm sorry. You didn't need to see that."

"Are you okay?" Again, as before, she reached out to touch him and, again, his heart stilled. How could one light touch convey so much? Or was he reading more into it than she meant?

"Evan?" she whispered his name. "Is everything okay?"

He couldn't speak at first. Then he swallowed the emotion, letting it recede.

All the while, Libby waited in silence.

He cleared his throat. "I wish it was, but it's not."

She did not move. She searched his face. What did she hope to find? He couldn't bear her scrutiny. So innocent. So sweet. Yet, so out of his reach. He drew his eyes away from her and stared down the hall.

"You can go to the chapel if you'd like time to yourself." The warmth of her hand on his arm left him.

"I don't want to be by myself." Why did his voice sound like the frightened little boy his father always brought out in him—the child that buried himself so far into the closet that his father couldn't find him when the torment of his family began? One day, Nate had found him. And Evan had paid for all the other days he'd remained hidden until his father's anger had passed.

Libby looked in the direction of the chapel. "I could go with you if you'd like."

He should head back to his office, but he wouldn't. Not if he could spend time with her. He nodded and followed her.

The chapel was empty. He sat beside her on the first

of the three pews in the small room. "You must love him very much," she spoke in hushed tones.

He held the cross in his hands and stared down at it. "No, Libby. I don't love him, but the victory is, I don't hate him anymore either."

She didn't flinch, and again, she placed her hand on his arm. No one in his life ever touched him with such tenderness.

Where in the world did such innocence receive such strength?

From her Center.

Her beautiful green eyes behind her glasses showered him with compassion like he'd never known. "I used to hate my father, too. Someday I'd like to tell him I've forgiven him, although I know he doesn't care. He left my mother and me when we needed him the most, and he never looked back."

"My father didn't leave. We would have been better off if he had. I have three brothers, and each of us carry our own scars. Joey's wife left him because of the violence; Ted turned to drugs, and Cody has shrugged off all sense of responsibility. I tried to help him, but the last I heard he's living on the streets of L.A."

"And what scars do you carry?" Her words were bold, but after she asked, she looked down at her hands.

The cross at the podium begged for his attention. He stared at it. If he told her, would she run? If she did leave him, never to look back, wouldn't it be better for her?

"You don't have to tell me. I shouldn't have asked."

He needed to share the ugly truth—give her the

chance to escape his grasp. Yet, he laid his hand over hers. "I'm an alcoholic, Libby." If the truth he'd shared about his alcoholism didn't close the doors, Evan was sure if Libby ever saw the mangled flesh on his back, she'd run as far away from him as possible. And never had he ached so badly at the thought of rejection.

But Libby didn't pull away, didn't even flinch at his announcement—a good sign. Nor did she give him a look of repulsion or of condemnation. She showed no discomfort with the conversation.

"One night, I got into my car alone and smashed it into a light pole. I was arrested, and the next day I stood before our mutual friend Judge Gideon. He took the time to ask me about myself and discovered that I'd done it on purpose. At the speed I hit that pole, I didn't expect to survive, but there I was standing in handcuffs with barely a scratch on me. Gideon knew what I'd lose with a DUI conviction and a three-day trip to the mental hospital, so he issued a challenge to me and to the assistant state attorney. If I cleaned up, started attending AA meetings or something similar, and if I agreed to speak to high school students about the dangers of drinking, drugs, and driving while under the influence, he'd expect the state attorney's office to offer a plea to reckless driving and drop the DUI."

"How long had you been drinking?"

"I started in high school and continued through college and into my career. When I wasn't drinking, I came across as a normal, everyday person. I worked hard in school and partied on the weekend. I started my first job, started my business, all handling the grind Monday through Friday and making everyone believe I was someone I wasn't."

Her luscious dark brows arched toward her delightful little nose. "I'm not sure I understand. If you weren't drinking, weren't you the person you needed to be, unhindered by substances."

"It's hard to explain." He offered her a smile that faded quickly. "My father's abuse left me empty. I mean, nothing. Maybe darkness. I acted like someone who cared, but inside I was a shell. I didn't feel anything." He studied his hands, trying to think of the right words. "The alcohol got me into plenty of fights. I didn't understand this before Christ filled that emptiness inside, but those brawls I got myself into covered the hole in my soul with wrath. My dad turned his anger on me and made me think of myself as a coward. To cope I shut those feelings out. Anger gave me the kind of control my father had over me, and the alcohol and drugs fueled my addiction to anger."

Why did he feel it so important to give Libby all the bad history? To get it out of the way so he could get to know her better? Or to make her run as fast and as far as she could from the monster he might still lay dormant inside him?

"Anger's a powerful emotion. It's fueled by more and more of the same, and it takes on a life of its own. I can't imagine how powerful your wrath could have been when you added the drugs and the alcohol."

Libby was a wise woman. He had nothing to say to

her sound reasoning.

"I've never taken a drink," she said. "Was it hard for you to give it up?"

He didn't think he'd ever met anyone who'd never had so much as a single beer. "I nearly stumbled once. A friend asked me to go to a party with her. I thought I could handle it. I couldn't. Even went so far as to pour myself a drink, but I set it down and stared at it from across the room all night. I've stayed away from temptation since then."

"With pride comes shame."

Evan smiled. "Something like that. Well, exactly like that."

"So, what happened with your DUI charge?"

"I bonded out of jail after my initial appearance and went back to Gideon's chambers to thank him. He welcomed me like an old friend, not like a criminal who'd just stood in front of him. He spent some time talking with me, and he recommended a Christian program for alcoholics. I didn't even balk at the thought. I was so desperate to feel more than hatred and rage that I followed through and so did Gideon.

"After my sentencing, I continued with the church meetings, and I checked in weekly with Gideon who, by default, became my accountability partner and later, he led me to Christ. I continue to speak in high schools when I get the chance."

Libby nodded, and for the first time he watched emotion cross her face. The gaze meeting his held compassion.

"Don't feel sorry for me, Libby. I'm one blessed man. It's only when Nate brings up my mother that I have to turn a truckload of bitterness over to God."

"Nate didn't …?"

"Kill her? Physically he tried, but spiritually, yeah. She's dead though. Cancer. She died a year ago." He could elaborate, but he didn't want to completely lose his composure in front of her.

"My mother died this year." Libby bowed her head and stared at her hands clasped in her lap. "She'd been sick most of my life."

His ailing mother had been with him for three months. He couldn't imagine a lifetime of health care. He was glad Libby shared, though. He wanted to know everything about her.

"But that's me." Libby turned with a trembling smile on her face. "We're talking about you. So, you're taking care of Nate. I know it must be hard."

She was wrong. He only wanted to talk about her. "Hard isn't the word."

She stood. "I'm going to leave you now, because I think you need to take your cares to the Lord. He'll soothe your heart much better than my unintelligent words. I'll remember to pray for you, and I'll thank God I've met a new friend who sacrifices for someone he feels doesn't deserve it."

Evan reached out and grasped her hand. Hearing the quick intake of breath, he knew he startled her. "I'll thank God I've met a friend who cares enough to direct me to the Lord when she doesn't have the solution."

"God is always the solution, Evan. Always." She slipped from his grasp and moved to the door, opened it, and stopped. A shy smile adorned her beautiful face. "Go to Him. I know He's filled that emptiness with His Spirit Who longs to comfort you now."

She left, and he bowed his head in silent prayer. At first, the words didn't come, and he simply drew before the Lord and listened.

Not rendering evil for evil, or railing for railing: but contrariwise blessing; knowing that ye are thereunto called, that ye should inherit a blessing.

The verse surfaced from the innermost part of his mind, and he recalled the pastor's sermon the week prior. The force of it spurred him to shame. "I know. I know, Lord. Nate is my heritage. The broken pieces of me are all he has left. In Your strength they will be enough."

He rose from the pew and with one last look toward the cross on the podium, he left the chapel. The backward glance caused him to sidestep an elderly woman in a wheelchair. "Excuse me, ma'am."

"Quite all right." She smiled up at him, making him feel as if he'd been left out of a joke. "Have a good day," she called.

"Thank you." Evan waved. "You, too."

All Evan wanted was to get out of this place where death lingered with life and where he could never forget that he was the son of a monster.

Chapter Three

The nursery needed work. Libby stood in the garden portion of the property and surveyed the acreage. Her eyes rested on the roof of the nursery's shop where obvious water damage had occurred. The hot house behind the shop stood solid. Of course, it needed a good cleaning, but she was up to the task. Those problems didn't bother her. She dug her bare hands into the sandy soil and let it sift through her hands. She'd need to put some nutrients into the ground.

Gideon and Evan plundered through the cottage-like shop. Their footsteps thundered over the wooden flooring, muffling the murmuring of their voices—Gideon's baritone and Evan's equally masculine tone.

Charisse came from the other side of the grounds. "Libby, this place seems more and more wonderful each time we visit."

"I hope the men reach the same conclusion. Without their okay, I won't move forward." Libby straightened, wiping the dirt from her hands. "God has given me wise counselors."

"We're going to check out the hot house, Lib," Gideon announced, and he and Evan headed from the cottage to the other building.

Libby pushed down her questions. She would wait,

letting them examine the place thoroughly. Her gaze met Evan's. Her heart embraced the smile he sent her way before the two men disappeared into the building.

Libby smoothed a lock of hair from her face and turned to Charisse. "How well do you know Evan?"

"Gideon and Evan know each other through Gideon's work."

Always discreet. Charisse said only what needed to be said, and Libby appreciated that.

"He's a member of our church." Charisse wiped her hands on her jeans. "Which you would know if you'd stop driving to Titusville every Sunday and Wednesday." Charisse nudged her. "I bet if I'd told you he was attending, I could have wooed you to church with me."

"It's hard to give up the church family I've known all my Christian life, and Charisse, I'm glad I didn't know. Now you've put temptation in my head. I won't know if …" She stopped at Charisse's wide grin.

"Caught ya." Charisse pointed. "I've been waiting for you to tell me how you felt about Evan since I noticed you watching his every move each morning."

So Charisse had noticed her observation of Evan, but for how long, and had her friends snared the poor man in a trap to introduce him to her? Libby didn't care. He was here and not sitting two tables away reading a newspaper and drinking his coffee—black. Oh yeah, she had it bad. She smiled. "Charisse, he's wonderful."

Charisse, her forehead wearing a crease, touched Libby's shoulder. "Be careful, okay? Don't let your heart blind you to his imperfections." She turned her gaze to the greenhouse and back to Libby. "Will you ask Gideon the same question you asked me?"

Libby's smile vanished, and her mood slipped from ecstasy to disappointment. She searched her memory. What had she asked? Oh, Evan. "Is there anything wrong?"

"There are portions of Evan's life that for me to say anything would seem like gossip."

"And from Gideon?"

"Even he might ask you to speak to the source."

"I know his …" Libby bit her tongue. She almost fell into the trap of declaring information Evan might not want known. She wouldn't betray his trust so easily.

"But you really like him, don't you?" Charisse raised her eyebrows up and down.

Warmth seeped into Libby's face. "He's so nice. Don't you think?"

"Libby, he's a great guy. Gideon and I would be so happy if he turned out to be the one." Charisse stepped closer. "Despite all our attempts at matchmaking, we know you've never been involved with anyone. These great feelings I see boiling over in you can scald a heart. I don't want that to happen."

Libby tensed at her words and the implication they held for her. "I'm an inexperienced little nobody and what would an experienced, handsome man like Evan Carter see in me?" She pushed her glasses up on her face.

"Wow." Charisse leaned away from her.

Libby swallowed hard, pushing down a knot of pride.

She sighed. "I'm sorry."

"You're not a little nobody. You're the most special somebody I know. Besides my man"—she hitched her thumb in Gideon's direction as the two men exited the hot house—"you're my best friend. I want you to have a relationship like the one Gideon and I share."

Libby shook her head. She had to get Charisse and her husband off the matchmaking track. "Listen to us talk as if I'm looking for a someone to complicate my life. I have too much going on now, don't you think?"

The men stepped outside, and Libby breathed a sigh of relief that Charisse would not be able to challenge her.

Gideon's cell phone rang with the familiar University of Florida Fightin' Gator song. "Hey, Veej. Yeah, Mommy's here. You okay? Are you behaving for Mamaw? I miss you. We'll pick you up tomorrow morning. Here's Mommy."

Gideon handed the phone to Charisse. She walked away from them, talking to her son.

"I love that kid," Gideon spoke of his stepson. "The adoption goes through in a few weeks."

"That's great," Evan smiled. "How'd he vote to change his name?"

Evan was closer to Gideon than Charisse let on. Gideon didn't speak of his family to everyone, only those he trusted and loved.

"Vance Wellman Tabor." Gideon beamed. "He keeps his dad's first and last name and takes on my last name."

"That boy never ceases to amaze me." Libby shook her head. "He could teach adults a thing or two about moving forward."

"Vance Wellman left me a wonderful family."
Gideon smiled and then tweaked Libby's nose. "Including
you."

Charisse ended the call and stepped back to rejoin the
group. "Okay, the suspense is killing me, guys. I'm sure
Libby's anxious, too. Give us the scoop."

Gideon shielded his eyes from the setting sun. "Let's
get out of the heat and into a restaurant before we start
this conversation."

"Gideon Tabor." Charisse gave him a playful slap to
his arm.

"Woman, submit to your husband." Gideon wrapped
her in an embrace and started toward their car.

Libby lifted her gaze to Evan. What would it be like
to have someone who interacted with such love and
compatibility? Watching them, she'd almost forgotten
that they'd picked her up and given her a ride to the
nursery.

"Want to ride with me?" Evan asked.

Libby weighed the question. The very thought of
being alone with him in his truck scared her to death. Her
heart fell then soared in synchronization with her nod.

Libby waited as Evan picked up the newspapers and
other junk thrown about his truck. He tossed them into the
back of the cab. "Sorry. This cab is my second office, and

I'm a bit messy."

Libby smiled and said nothing about the clutter or the dirt on his floorboard. After all Evan worked in construction. His truck and the things inside of it seemed a natural part of him. He helped her up into the king-size cab and closed the door. Going around to the other side, he jumped in and started the truck. The big diesel engine roared to life. Libby fastened her seatbelt, and he did the same.

"I've never ridden in a truck like this before." Libby opened the conversation. "They do sit up high, don't they?"

Evan nodded as he pulled behind Gideon. He hunted for something in a stack, and with a smile, he pulled out a box of wet wipes. "I like to have these on hand." He tugged one out of the box and handed it to her and then grabbed one for himself.

"You must have decided on a restaurant." She wiped the nursery's sand from her hands.

Evan opened a bag with other papers and wrappers inside. "Just toss it in there."

Libby wadded the wipe and put it in the bag.

"We're going to 310 Lakeside. Gideon said you haven't lived in Orlando long. Have you ever been?"

"No." Libby gulped. This wasn't a simple dinner out. This was fine dining in downtown Orlando. "Am I dressed okay?"

His brown eyes took her in.

She squirmed under the scrutiny.

"You look beautiful." He cleared his throat. "Gideon

said you always wear nice things. He didn't lie. I'm the one in jeans, but they'll let me in."

He thought she was beautiful—or he said it anyway. Truth or not, she was warmed by his words. No man had ever said that about her.

Gideon told him she always dressed nicely. Libby straightened. Only the day before she'd mentioned to Charisse how beautiful the place looked from the outside, and how nice it would be to dine there.

She wanted so badly to roll down the window, afraid she'd begin sweating from her embarrassment. Her stomach rolled as she stared at her hands clasped in her lap. She'd actually told Charisse it would be a nice place to go for a first date. Charisse must have known she was thinking of Evan when she said it. Libby had not kept her secret from her best friend, and Charisse and Gideon were definitely taking advantage of Evan. She squeezed her hands together.

"Everything okay?" The unsuspecting victim asked her.

Libby swallowed past the lump in her throat. She could only nod.

"Libby, I—" The ring of his cell phone cut off their conversation. "Evan Carter."

What was he about to say to her? Was it the "I only want to be friends" speech? At least she'd finally gotten that far with a guy.

Evan's conversation ensued until they reached the restaurant. "Sorry." He put the phone down. "Client."

When Evan opened her door, Libby accepted the offer of his arm as she prepared to climb from the monster vehicle. Stepping down, she looked into Evan's eyes and decided that a more handsome man never existed on the face of the earth. Granted, she had very limited experiences, but no one set her mind to reeling the way Evan did.

"Gid and Charisse have already gone inside," he noted.

She followed him and waited as he held open the door for her. Once inside she made her way through the small crowd to where Charisse stood waiting for Gideon to place their names on the waiting list. The aroma of charbroiled steaks seasoned with peppercorn teased Libby's appetite.

Evan stood beside her. A departing couple tried to push their way to the door. Evan slipped his arm around Libby's shoulders and brought her closer to him. The couple passed, but Evan's arm still held her so close she could smell the spice in his cologne. Libby fought the shiver of delight. She never wanted to move nor did she want Evan to release her.

"Ten minutes," Gideon announced upon his return. "Why don't we sit and wait?"

No. Libby's heart screamed as Evan's warmth left her. He waited until Libby and Charisse sat on the long bench. Once they settled in the middle both men sat on either side of them.

Libby gazed out the window at the blue heavens highlighted in the oranges and pinks of a sun departing for the day. Her heart pounded, begging for Evan's touch—just once more.

"I suppose we'll have to wait until we get seated to hear your evaluation of Libby's nursery." Charisse gave her husband a playful smirk.

As smoothly as he'd done before, Evan slipped his arm around Libby and leaned forward to see Charisse. "I think so. You're more impatient than the prospective owner."

If Libby wanted to be honest, she would admit that he rested his arm in a natural gesture, but the alternative made her silly heart sing, and she didn't want to let go of the fantasy.

"I know how much this means to her." Charisse's gaze cut to Evan's arm around Libby.

"Well," Gideon remarked. "Rest assured I wouldn't let Libby worry if the news wasn't mostly good."

"That's reassuring, huh?" Charisse asked.

Evan settled back beside her, and Libby could think of nothing else besides his touch and the smell of his cologne. She closed her eyes and drank in the spicy scent, allowing herself to dream of his lips touching hers. The image surprised her as much as the sudden sound of Evan's name on another woman's lips.

Evan stood so abruptly the movement jarred Libby. She opened her eyes and beheld the woman Delilah had introduced her to only that morning at Java Lava—Hope Astor—and an angry glare darkened Hope's beautiful, but hostile, blue eyes.

"Good to see you." Hope's tone betrayed her lie. She wasn't happy to see any of them, including Evan.

Libby wasn't sure, but Evan seemed to be maneuvering in front of her.

"What a surprise." Another beautiful woman joined the exquisite blonde. "Hey, Evan." She practically bounced from excitement, apparently at seeing an old friend. "Hope was just saying we might see you at Christa's party."

Gideon stood and pulled Charisse with him. Libby followed, but Evan moved so as to keep Libby from view. He introduced first the blonde, "Hope," then "Tiffany. Old friends."

"I think we're more than old friends, Evan." Hope pushed between them, knocking Libby back even further. Hope looped her arm with Evan's and turned to shoot invisible daggers toward Libby, each one piercing Libby's heart. "And who is your new friend?"

They'd only met that morning, but Libby remembered her. Was this woman playing games or was she really so shallow she could have forgotten already?

Evan turned. He stared at Libby for a moment, appearing to hesitate. "Libby … Libby … I don't remember her last name."

"Libby Overstreet." Charisse's voice bristled with irritation.

Libby tucked her emotions away for later. With the sound of Gideon's name called by the hostess, Libby gave a silent prayer of thanks to the Lord for His intervention.

She slipped around Hope without a word. She never

liked to be rude, but not even a twinge of guilt consumed her. She followed Charisse and Gideon to their table and wondered if Evan would choose the beautiful women over their company.

Chapter Four

Evan parked the truck in his driveway and sat in the darkness. Crickets chirped and doves cooed in the trees surrounding his home. On any other evening he would be sitting alone on his back porch listening to the sounds of life around him: nocturnal creatures scampering in the leaves, bull gators in the lake sending out their croaking love sonnet, and the old owl in the hundred year old oak asking, "Who? Who?"

For the last few weeks, the answer to the owl's question would have been "Libby," though he hadn't known her name to provide it to the wise old fellow in the tree. Yet the beautiful brunette with the piercing green eyes was all he could think of except when he immersed himself in work, and even then, a vision of her sweet face tempted him away for brief snatches of daydreams.

He pulled the door handle and kicked the heavy truck door open. If it fell back on him, a broken leg would serve him right.

Libby … Libby … I don't remember her last name.

"Lord, why did I have to hurt her—with my words, no less? From the look on her face, I might as well have punched her in the stomach."

Before his blunder, when he'd put his arms around her, he knew he wanted to get to know this girl better. At first, he meant it only as a friendly gesture to guide her out of the path of others, but when she looked up at him through those oversized glasses, she'd ensnared him with her genuineness. It seemed as if God had placed Libby in his path, not only once but three times in one day. Anyone would have taken that for confirmation on God's part.

Then God had brought Evan's past back to him, not with a memory, but in a face-to-face encounter with Hope and Tiffany.

No, he had not forgotten Libby's name. When Gideon had introduced him to her, Libby Overstreet's name had been etched into his heart.

He'd had a gut reaction to seeing Hope. Without thinking of it, he'd moved to protect Libby from Hope's vindictive sarcasm. Instead, he'd made a terrible mess of things, and Evan wondered if what he thought of as confirmation was actually foolish thinking on his part.

He used to only worry that he would inherit Nate's propensity for physical violence. Not so. His father's most powerful weapon had been the way his words made you think you were less than who you really were in God's eyes. Evan had worked hard to overcome the voice of his father's loathing—the voice that had almost convinced him he wasn't good enough to live.

Evan had also worked very hard memorizing verses about the strength of the tongue and avoiding speech that God condemned. He tried to be so careful with his words, but he'd hurt Libby just the same.

Libby didn't have to utter a word. Cellophane covered the brave front she presented, and he could see straight into her vulnerable heart. And those precious lips, they'd quivered once or twice when the dinner conversation waned—and it had waned.

Libby was a fragile, beautiful butterfly, and he crushed her with his brutish and ugly nature.

He made certain the truck's heavy door slammed with ferocity before making his way down the mulched path to his home. As he fumbled for the key and opened the door, his phone rang. A flip of the switch bathed the living room in light. The caller ID announced Hope wanted to talk. The flashing light told him she'd left other messages. The more she drank tonight, the more frequent the calls would come.

He pushed the off button for the answering machine and waited for her to give up. Throwing his keys on the table, he moved toward the kitchen for a glass of tea.

Before he reached the refrigerator, he leaned against the wall. "Lord," he cried out and then fell silent. He wanted to ask God for Libby despite the fact he didn't deserve her. "Will my past sins separate me from her? I thought I was as broken as a man can get. Then I saw Libby. I ruined it, Lord. I hurt her." Again, he grew still before God, unable to put his feelings into words but desperately wanting God to open a door for him.

The phone rang, and Evan swallowed down his anger with Hope. Would she ever leave him alone? The ringing continued. He reached over and snatched up the receiver. "Yeah?"

"Listen, I just have a second to tell you this while the

girls are doing whatever girls do when they go to the restroom together."

"Gid?"

"Yeah. Jot this number down. You owe Libby an apology, and you need to call her tonight."

Evan scrambled to the kitchen counter and grabbed a pen from the caddy. "I'm ready."

Gideon recited the number, and Evan wrote it down, repeating the sequence.

"Don't mess this one up. You got me?"

"I do."

"You hurt a good woman tonight—the best you'll ever find."

"I know. She's too good for me." The pain of truth left a slash in his heart.

"Yeah, well, Charisse is too good for me, but look at the man I've become, and if you ever tell Charisse I called about this, I'll reinstate your probation. We took Libby out for ice cream to keep her mind off your stupidity. Give us thirty minutes to get her home. Gotta go. Here they come. Say, has any man ever learned why they go to the bathroom in pairs?"

Libby trudged up the stairs to her apartment with her friends behind her. Gideon and Charisse had insisted on walking her to the door. The traffic on the highway rushed by. Libby had gotten used to the race of motors and the squeal of tires, but as they neared the door of her upstairs apartment, she realized tonight would be a long night, and the traffic would add to it.

She placed her key into the lock. "Would you like to come in?" Politeness dictated the question.

"Libby, listen, Evan didn't mean it the way it sounded." Gideon leaned against the wall.

Libby straightened and pushed a smile into place. She didn't need this now. "Thank you for asking him to look at the old place. He seems very good at what he does, and I appreciate the advice."

"I just don't want you to feel hurt." He tilted his head and gave her that little-boy look that Charisse often told Libby she'd fallen in love with long ago.

"Hurt? What on earth could he have done to hurt me? I just met him." What a terrible liar she'd become.

"Libby, what Gideon is trying to tactfully say is that Evan treated you badly tonight."

"I'm not trying to say that," Gideon protested. "You women think you have us men all figured out." He pushed from the wall now. "So what if Evan didn't know or remember your last name. Big deal. Libby, the guy is topnotch. Don't hold his lapse of memory against him."

Charisse brushed Libby's curls from her face. Libby stepped away from her reach. She wasn't a small child in need of a hug. "I'm fine, you two. Go home. You're making a big fuss about nothing. The guy looked at some property for me, and you would think I've picked out my wedding gown."

Gideon reached over and messed her hair with his big

paw. "You might not have picked it out yet, but I think Charisse has. She might also have the wedding chapel rented."

Charisse rammed an elbow into her husband's ribs. "I hadn't gotten that far. I only just started thinking of color combinations and how Gideon and I would pay for your honeymoon."

They were trying to make her laugh when she only wanted to cry. "I've always dreamed of a black and white wedding, and I've always wanted to visit Tahiti, but if Tahiti is too expensive, New Zealand is my second choice." She kept a straight face, but it took heroic effort to hold the tears at bay.

Gideon's laughter pealed like a gong against the air, and Charisse kissed her cheek. "When the right man comes along, you can count on us."

"Black and white wedding, huh?" Gideon rubbed his chin. "What color are the flowers, black or white?"

"Red roses," Libby's voice chorused with Charisse's.

"Well, Charisse has obligated us. When the time comes, Liberty *Overstreet*, the wedding and the honeymoon are on us."

The likelihood of their having to pay off was nil, but Libby nodded. "Thank you so much for all you've done for me today." She put her key in the lock and turned it. "See you for coffee tomorrow, Charisse?"

"Bright and early."

Libby slipped inside and stood with her back against the door, listening until her friends' banter faded. The darkness of her apartment enveloped her. "I am so stupid to have believed he could ever be interested in me." She moved through her apartment and sat on the couch.

Loneliness had failed to visit her even following her mother's passing. The business of death kept her active, and afterward she focused on starting a new life. Now, though, solitude closed in on her. This rented apartment would never feel like a home. She should have kept the house she grew up in and never moved away from Titusville.

"Why did he treat me like he cared?" she asked the darkness. "Was it just my childish imagination?"

His touch had warmed her, made her feel important. His open rejection humiliated and devastated her, though she'd worked very hard to keep her emotions tamped down. Again, she managed to keep them from erupting. Who was here to hear her? God was here with her. She leaned her head back. "Dear Father, You know this pain and where it comes from. I trust You. You're the only One who knows." She could handle most anything thrown at her, but rejection left her beaten and bruised every time.

When Evan joined them at the table, he'd been distracted. He'd distanced himself from her. Well, why not? What a contrast between the belles he introduced to her and her own plain appearance. Those girls were dressed up, maybe a little too immodestly, but the difference between Libby and Hope Astor was the difference between the girl next door and a high-fashioned model. Libby didn't have a chance.

Evan had been anxious to finish dinner and get out of

there. He probably wanted to join up with his two friends, but at least he'd stayed to dine with Libby, Gideon and Charisse, and he refused to allow Libby—or Gideon—to pay the bill in return for his expertise at the nursery site.

The news Gideon and Evan had shared with her should have made her happy, but sitting at the restaurant table, she could barely look up as the two men explained that while the nursery would require some renovations, the bones of the buildings were quite sound. For some reason, the nursery and Evan became entangled in her mind. One without the other would not do.

She took off her glasses and rubbed her eyes. She stared at the large plastic and unfashionable frames, and heat flamed her cheeks. Before this moment, she'd jokingly referred to them as "Libby-style." Now, they embarrassed her. Even Libby-style had not been enough to make her memorable to Evan.

Evan might not remember Libby's name, but she would never forget the name of the other woman who'd destroyed her momentary dreams.

Hope. Her name was Hope.

She'd heard the anger and derision behind Hope's snide remarks, heard Evan's stuttering admission that she wasn't even important enough for him to remember her last name.

He'd only been nice to her because she was a friend of Gideon's. And, though, she'd never admit this to her two friends, they had been right. Her heart practically had them married and on the way to Tahiti. How foolish could one inexperienced woman get? She had to get her feet firmly planted in the land of reality.

"Lord, I got all wrapped up in my feelings for Evan and forgot to look to You for my peace and comfort. Rejection hurts, Lord, but I placed myself in the position this time. I opened myself up for the hurt because I took my eyes off of you." She'd not only been rejected by Evan, but Hope's disdain cut deep into her soul. "I've never felt this way about a man, Lord. Help me to let these feelings go. Show me what am I to do that will glorify You?"

She stood and turned on the lights, and still the apartment didn't seem as bright as usual. The entire place seemed so tiny. "I want to go home, Lord. I want to undo everything I've done." But she couldn't. The choices she'd made were permanent ones. She'd had such high hopes of a new life. Liberty Overstreet was free to chase her dreams—the dreams her mother made her promise she'd pursue.

And for a few weeks, Libby had even been foolish to believe that God might just stave her loneliness with a man who, even before she knew his name, touched her deeply.

Enough of that. She'd prayed. She needed to move on.

The phone rang. She ignored it until the persistent jangling cut through her last nerve. "Hello."

"Libby?"

Libby closed her eyes and collapsed back against the kitchen counter.

"Libby Overstreet? Gideon gave me this number."

"Evan. Hello."

"Are you okay?"

"I'm fine. How can I help you?" She covered her eyes with her hand.

"Ouch."

"Ouch? What do you mean?" She lowered her hand.

"I guess I shouldn't expect any kindness from you."

Libby winced. "Evan, I'm sorry. Did I sound curt? I didn't mean to. You deserve every consideration. You went out of your way for me this afternoon, and I appreciate your help very much. This is my dream after all."

"Hope …" he said and stopped.

If Hope entered Libby's dream, it would become a nightmare. The sound of her name from his lips snuffed out any delusions his phone call might have rekindled. Still, she needed to remain polite. "Yes, Hope. I know I treated her badly. I'm glad you called. I want to apologize to you, and I certainly owe Hope an apology if I see her again."

Libby heard his sharp intake of breath. "I pray you never get that opportunity."

Well, at least they were on the same wavelength, but had her behavior been so terrible that Evan wanted to protect Hope from her?

"You and Hope are not in the same league," Evan answered her thoughts.

The truth hurt. "I know."

"Libby, you're a sweet girl."

As with Charisse's brushing back of her hair and Gideon's mussing it, she felt like a child. "You don't have to explain it to me, Evan. I mean, we just met this morning. You did me a favor, and I appreciate it."

"And I appreciate what you did for me, too."

She'd done nothing for him, at least not anything she could recall. "Just the same, I know you're a busy man with more to do than take care of my needs. I'm sorry if I caused trouble between you and Hope." Libby bit her lip and covered the receiver as she fought to keep her emotions intact.

"I made a promise to you. I'm keeping it. When you close on the property, I'll get a crew over there right away."

She'd seen him from afar for weeks, but she'd known him for less than twenty-four hours. If she allowed it, her heart would begin to betray her with thoughts of love, and her brain would leave reality once again. She took a deep breath and released her dream to the Lord. "Evan, I don't think that's a good idea."

"I'd really like to help you realize your dream."

"That's so wonderful of you. I really do appreciate it, but I know that Gideon and Charisse put you up to everything, and I'm sorry that they involved you. You're a busy man. I can't hold you to this."

"I have resources. I'd really like to help you."

He seemed so adamant, but she just couldn't do it to him. Saying yes would allow her imagination to continue to deceive her into believing there was hope for her with this man. He'd be close enough to touch, and Libby had learned that Evan's touch burned.

"Just tell me you'll think this over. Give me a week. Seeing the place gave me some ideas. I'd like to sketch them out for you."

"Evan, please don't waste your time." She gripped the phone so hard her fingers ached. "I—I have to go now. Please have a good night." Libby hung up the phone.

Gideon and Charisse meant well, but she wouldn't allow Evan to waste any additional time on her. Neither would she be able to tell him that she'd decided to hire another contractor.

She'd just have to forget about the nursery.

Chapter Five

The door loomed between Libby and her visit with Nate Carter. What would she do if she found Evan sitting on the other side? The door to Nate's room opened, and Libby stepped back.

"Ah, you are here again, Miss Libby." A nurse exited, giving Libby a gentle touch on the shoulder.

Libby offered a glimmer of a smile. "Is he alone?"

"Yes and he has his nose buried in that there television. He's been asking about you, child." The woman's dark eyes bore into hers. "You be a watchin' him now. He's been a feisty fellow this week."

She always saved Nate's visit for last, hoping to avoid Evan. Both here and at the coffee shop, she'd successfully evaded him since their phone conversation a week before. Yet, she yearned for one glance of his handsome face.

The nurse stared at her, though Libby couldn't remember a word she'd said. A twinkle lit the woman's brown eyes. "His son's been a askin' after you, too. Quite a good looker, that one."

What could Libby say? "Thank you." She entered the dimly lit room. Very little sound came from the television as she crept inside. Nate sat in bed, his knuckles white from the grip he held on the remote. His mouth moved in unintelligible words.

Libby turned to see what held his rapt attention. Bombs exploding and bodies of men bloodied from the battle lay across her line of vision. She swallowed down the bile that would burn her throat. She'd never been allowed to watch these types of movies in her mother's home, and she had no taste for them now.

"Mr. Carter," she whispered. "It's Libby. Evan's friend." On two occasions, he hadn't remembered her. Would he remember her today? Even if he'd asked about her moments before, he was likely to forget soon after.

Nate's lips continued moving as he turned his steely gaze upon her. His words, almost unheard at first, reached her ears with a thunderous roar. "Evan is a no-good coward. He's a momma's boy. I tried to make a man of him, but he fought it all the way. He took her in, you know, after she left me."

Libby's heart wrenched in her chest. Nate spoke of his wife and son with such hatred. "Evan cares for you, Mr. Carter."

Nate turned back to the television screen where bombs continued to detonate, machine guns slaughtered, and men moaned in agony. Libby forced her sight away from the butchering and moved toward the door. She'd have to visit Nate another day.

Dishes clamored and silverware clanged. Libby spun. The items once atop Nate's food tray were strewn across his bed and onto the floor. His fist fell hard against the bed desk, his eyes boring into her with open hatred.

He sprang from the bed. Anger stormed in his

reddened face as he advanced upon her. "Mr. Carter." She held up her hands, backing away.

"Don't ever take up for that no-good kid. He betrayed me. Turned soft. All of them turned soft on me."

Nate stood over her, leaning closer and closer. His body stunk of sweat.

Libby fell backward against the opposite bed. She turned and scrambled for the call button, her hand grasping the small cord. Nate's strong grip fell around her wrist, wrenching her arm behind her back. Her shoulder popped and excruciating pain radiated through her arm. Vile curse words gushed from his lips. Libby cringed as his hot breath, dank with the smell of mashed potatoes and chopped steak, lingered against her neck. He yanked her arm upward.

"Oh," Libby screamed. "Mr. Carter, please." She fought to free herself. With each move, a fire raged up her arm and into her shoulder. He obviously meant to hurt her.

He continued to put pressure on her arm. The bed rolled. Struggling to stay upright, she moved with the bed. Another screamed pealed from her lips as pain stabbed her like a scorching poker.

A blow hit the middle of her back, forcing the air from her lungs, air she desperately needed, air she couldn't get back into her. She gulped, but the life force seemed to hang just outside her mouth and her nose.

Angry voices and light filled the room. Then came a loud clamor. Nate's curses turned to groans of pain. Each sound began to fade into the distance as darkness enveloped her. Her body floated on air, and a man whispered her name.

"Evan," she moaned as blackness, like a cloak, covered her.

Evan paced the waiting room while Gideon stared out into the night sky. Evan had called Gideon and Charisse as he sped after the ambulance.

The nursing home would attribute Nate's insane action to the Alzheimer's, but they were wrong. Nate had always been mean. Alzheimer's didn't bring on the demons his father harbored. They were always there, lingering beneath the surface, ready to pounce on anyone Nate imagined had crossed him.

Evan couldn't imagine anything Libby could have done to incite such madness.

"Settle down, Ev." Gideon turned from the window.

Evan paced a few more times then moved back to face his friend. "She tried to blow me off, Gideon. I thought at first it was because of my stupidity at the restaurant, but Libby genuinely seemed to think she'd been rude to Hope. That just endeared me to her, but the more I think about it, I realized Libby probably thought about what I'd shared with her about my past. She couldn't want me. No woman in their right mind should."

Gideon shook his head. "That gal is stronger than you think. Your past and the fact that you're overcoming it would endear you to her."

"If that's really true, then you have to realize that's why I can't see her."

"Care to explain that one to me a little more thoroughly. I'm not getting the connection."

"She's like my mother. She'll try to rationalize every wrong thing I do."

"So you won't do *those* wrong things. Sure you'll mess up once in a while, but Evan, your faith is lacking."

"I'm trying to protect Libby from the kind of violence she experienced at my father's hands. Now, can you and Charisse understand why I can't let my feelings for Libby hurt her? Will you stop pestering me about it now?" Not that he hadn't been swayed by their pestering. He'd been able to think of little besides Libby.

"Seems to me she got hurt without you and not by you. Your father is not you." Gideon looked down at his folded hands.

"That's my legacy, Gideon. That's what I could do to her. She's so much like my mother. Libby thinks the best of everyone, and I'm—"

"The Son of Frankenstein's monster. Your father isn't responsible for his actions. He's out there somewhere in a world all his own."

Evan clawed at his t-shirt, raising it high on his back. He turned so that Gideon could get a good look at the full extent of his father's cruelty. "I'm pretty sure he had all his faculties when he did this to me."

Evan waited while Gideon examined the raised, wide

scars across Evan's back. He closed his eyes almost believing he could feel the heated bar searing into his skin six times—a special retribution for a coward who hid in closets. He'd almost died from the pain and the open blistery wounds before his father finally left the house for a long truck route. Only then could his mother get him to the hospital where they'd both lied about the injury. He'd fallen against an outdoor grill. Not that the doctors believed him or his mother, but what could they do? The hospital called in the police and children's services, but with three brothers and a mother confirming his story and saying that his father had been out of town, the case had been closed.

Gideon didn't have to say anything as he moved in front of Evan. The look in his friend's eyes spoke of the horror he imagined Evan had endured. Gideon would never know the half of it. Taking the pain yourself was less hurtful than watching the ones you love suffer. He'd never again hidden in the closet when his father went after his brothers or his mother. They may have been dysfunctional in every other way, but they all knew how to stand united while Nate chose which one he wanted to take the force of his anger. Evan always prayed that his father would hurt him. Watching Nate hurt the others was harder to bear than any pain his father inflicted upon him.

Evan yanked down his shirt. "My brothers have their own set of scars. Joey has burns on his neck and chest from a boiling pot of water." He stepped away from Gideon and stood in front of the candy vending machine. Instead of the sweets, the bitterness in his eyes peered at him from his own reflection in the glass. "She's all I think about. If God wanted to protect her, why did he send her across my path?"

"Maybe God knows Libby is what you need."

"But He'd be so kind to me and so cruel to her? It doesn't make sense. Stop playing matchmaker. She doesn't need a monster like me in her life."

"You're not a monster. If you were, you wouldn't be taking care of your dad the way you do. Evan, people learn from the mistakes of others. You're a successful man with a very good head on your shoulders. You also have Christ in your heart."

Evan leaned his head against the vending machine glass. "I didn't show Christ in me while nearly killing my father this evening."

"You wanted to protect Libby. It's only natural to act that way."

"Excuse me, boys, but I have a groggy little lady here who needs to get home and into bed." Charisse wheeled Libby through the emergency room door. "I may need both of you to help me."

Evan pushed away from the machine and drank in the sight of Libby. She sat in a wheelchair, her hair messed. Her eyes closed for long moments before she tried to open them. The over-round glasses he loved lay broken in her lap. A sling cradled her wrapped left arm.

Charisse pushed the chair forward.

"I'll get the car," Gideon called as he rushed off, leaving Evan to walk with the women.

"Evan."

He cringed at Charisse's whisper. She probably hated him. Nothing he didn't deserve.

"Do you care anything about her?"

How could she ask him that question? He should have lied, but instead he nodded.

"As much as I think you do?"

Again he nodded. "More."

"Then you fight your fears, and you make her dreams come true."

Libby's body slumped forward. Evan reached down to keep her from falling from the wheelchair.

"Poor thing. They gave her some strong painkillers." Charisse giggled and then covered her mouth. "I don't think she's ever taken anything like them."

Evan doubted it, too. A woman who never touched a drop of alcohol probably wouldn't reach for prescription drugs to deaden any pain—mental or physical.

God, I covet Libby's quiet strength. What a man couldn't do with her beside him.

Gideon's car approached. Evan bent down and scooped Libby into his arms. She cried out in pain.

"I'm sorry. I'm sorry." He held her against him.

"She has a big bruise on her back where he must have punched her." Charisse stroked Libby's hair.

"He's good at that punch."

Charisse opened the car door, and Evan sat in the back cradling Libby against him on his lap. Charisse slid in the front seat beside her husband. "Gideon will bring you back for your car."

Libby's lush eyelashes fell against her face. In her sleep, she winced.

"I'm so sorry. I'm so sorry." He'd say it a million times if the words would only take her hurt away. Could an apology do that? He wouldn't know. Nate never apologized for any of the pain he'd inflicted on others.

"Evan?" A soft sob escaped her lips.

"I'm here." He brushed her soft brown hair from her face.

"I'm so lonely."

Charisse turned in her seat to stare at him. "She's lonely for *you*."

"Charisse," Gideon admonished. "You're meddling."

Charisse flopped back down in her seat like a child after a scolding.

In the rearview mirror, Gideon winked at him.

Evan shook his head and looked down at Libby sleeping in his embrace. "I'm lonely, too," he whispered.

Libby fought against the grogginess to open her eyes. In the darkness of the room, she focused for a moment to see through the soft light before searching for something familiar. Nothing. The truth brought panic, and a sharp pain stabbed her arm and shoulder as she tried to push out of bed. "Nate," she whispered the older man's name through a mouth that felt as dry as cotton.

"Lib?"

Libby's eyes closed, but she forced them open. For the first time, Libby made out Charisse's silhouette in the chair beside her.

"How are you doing? Do you need anything?" Charisse leaned forward.

"How's Mr. Carter? I hope I didn't cause him to get hurt."

Charisse laughed. "Now I know you're okay. Even without those glasses, you still see the world with a rose tint. Nate is nursing the bruises he got when Evan pulled him away from you. He's under sedation, and the nurses have demanded restraints."

"Poor man." Libby shook her head. "Is Evan okay?" Again, her eyes tried to close, but she needed to hear Charisse's answer.

"Evan's fine. He's sleeping downstairs on the couch. Would you like me to wake him? He's anxious to see you."

She needed to see him. Her heart demanded it. Her mind, however, forced her to see the truth. Evan's life revolved around a world where she'd never fit, and now, she'd caused another difficulty in his life—his father's freedom had been affected by her stupidity. "Would you tell him I'm fine, and ask him to leave?"

"Libby, he's very worried about you."

"That's why you need to tell him I'm okay. His relationship with his father was bad enough. Now, look what I've done." She looked away from her friend.

"He cares about you."

"Stop it, Charisse. I'm tired of the nagging. Evan

isn't interested in me." She closed her eyes and allowed her tears to soak the pillow. "His poor father."

"You're not afraid of him because of his dad? The man was cruel to Evan's family."

"I didn't have to be with Evan for more than one day to realize he's not Nate. I love Evan because despite what Nate put Evan through, he's still taking care of his father."

Through the darkness, Libby could almost feel Charisse's stare.

"Libby?"

"Please. Ask him to leave."

Charisse patted Libby's good arm. "Let him sleep for a while. He's been up most of the night worried over you. He finally crashed about an hour ago. Maybe you'll change your mind in the morning."

"On what planet would I ever fit into Evan's world? We're two different people with two different lives."

"I hate to break this to you, kiddo, but if anyone ever found another somebody who lived the exact same life and acted the same way they did, the relationship would be a boring one."

Libby swallowed. She'd take a boring relationship any day. Boring sure beat the constant pang of loneliness.

The medication was making her emotional. That had to be it. She pinched her eyes closed and swiped away tears with her good hand.

"Libby, he's shared some sketches for the nursery. You need to look at them. If I didn't know better, I'd believe the man has known you his entire life. What he's depicted is so you."

"There won't be a nursery. Not one I own anyway. I gave up that dream, too." Libby tried to roll over but the pain was too much.

Her dreams and the nursery had placed her in the center of his life, and her run-in with Nate caused friction between Evan and his father. Evan was a nice man who'd been trapped into helping a little hapless nobody, and look what it cost him.

Chapter Six

Evan looked over the edge of his newspaper and stared at the two women in the corner. Java Lava was busy this morning but not too busy that he didn't see Libby immediately. He'd been hoping to run into her here for weeks. Gideon told him the girls met later than usual because Charisse had to drop V.J. at school. Evan believed the change in time was an avoidance tactic on Libby's part.

He stared at Libby's back. The sling still held her left arm tucked to her body, reminding him of all the reasons he shouldn't be here watching her and planning to talk to her, but he couldn't leave. His carelessness cost her so much. He needed to right all the wrongs.

Charisse's eyes met his a time or two, but she didn't give him away.

Evan skimmed over the latest news but retained none of it. He touched his shirt pocket to make sure one of his gifts for Libby remained tucked safely inside.

"Oh! I'm so sorry." Beside Libby, at another table, a woman spilled her coffee.

Libby pushed back, but the coffee had landed on her pretty flowered skirt. Evan sprang to his feet. The hot liquid must have burned.

Before he could get to her, Libby leaned down

toward the distraught elderly woman. "It's okay. It's okay." She offered a comforting hug with her good arm. "Accidents happen. I'm washable."

Evan smiled. So few people in his life were as gracious as Libby Overstreet.

"Let me get us something to clean this up." Libby patted the lady's shoulder. When she turned away, she closed her eyes in a deep wince, pulling the skirt off her skin and then shifting the sling. She pushed out air between her precious lips.

"Libby, are you okay?" Evan stepped toward her.

She stopped, staring at him through her new, modern glasses, as if he were a ghostly specter who'd appeared only to haunt her. Two waitresses scurried around them to clean up the mess.

"Are you okay?" he repeated, pulling Libby aside.

She half shook her head and half nodded. "Burned a little. That's all."

A glaring red mark dotted the top of her right hand where some of the coffee probably landed.

"How have you been?" Libby asked.

"I should be asking you that question. I owe you an apology. My father ..."

"Evan, you don't owe me a thing. You aren't responsible for what happened."

"Libby, he's a dangerous man. Always has been. I should have asked the nursing home to keep you away from him—to keep you safe."

Her pretty green eyes softened. "Really, it's okay."

He blinked. Did she realize how she mesmerized

him? He didn't want to talk about his father. He wanted to find a way to get back into her good graces despite his father. "I'm glad I ran into you here today. I have a special favor to ask you."

She straightened and again pulled the skirt away.

"But you're hurting. You probably need to go home and change, tend to—"

"No. I have a doctor's appointment in half an hour. I don't have time to drive back to my apartment. I'm sorry. You said something about a favor."

"Yeah, there's an art show at Harry P. Leu Gardens. No one else I know would enjoy both the talent and the flowers. I was hoping you might go with me."

"Evan, I don't think so."

The elderly woman hobbled up from her seat and toward them. "Darling, I'm so sorry. Young man, I didn't mean to do that to your dear wife."

Dear. Even strangers saw it in her.

Wife. Why did his chest ache at the word?

"Please take care." Libby nodded and then her gaze flitted to him for a brief second. Her cheeks reddened. "I'm sure the place is beautiful, but I'd better not."

"It would mean a lot to me."

She lowered her head. "Why me?"

Behind her, Charisse motioned him to keep going. And do what? Play on her sympathies?

"Why not you?" he asked and then backed away. "That's okay." He reached into his pocket and held out the folded paper. "It's just a sketch, but I wanted you to see a vision I had for your nursery. Maybe you can take a look at it, and if you want to change anything, I'd love to work on it with you. I have other plans drawn up. Tentative, of course, but I think we can make them work."

She held up her hand. "There is no nursery."

"Gideon …"

Charisse gave her head an adamant shake.

Libby turned to look at her friend and then gave Evan her full attention. "Gideon what?"

"Gideon said you haven't forfeited your escrow. He said the owner gave you more time to make a decision."

Libby took a deep breath and released it slowly, finishing with a deep sigh. "I don't want you wasting your time on me."

"You are not a waste of time." He reached for her hand. "Libby, if I did anything to hurt you so badly that you're even thinking of giving up your dreams, I'm sorry. You have to understand. I'm the one who isn't worth it. If you don't want me to be a part of it, that's fine. That's probably a very wise decision, but look at the sketch. See one possibility that could make your desires a reality." He pushed the paper at her, and finally she took it from him.

Her eyes softened, looking to him as if … He could almost believe he saw desire in her gaze.

He brushed the back of his hand against her cheek, her skin soft beneath his touch.

She leaned into his caress, closed her eyes, and breathed deeply.

What was he doing? He pulled back, clenching his fist. "Have a wonderful life, Libby Overstreet." He spun away from her, each step toward the door wrenching his heart.

"Evan?"

His name on her lips stopped him, but he didn't turn. The desire to see her one more time would have to burn inside. If he couldn't have her …

"When is the art exhibit?"

He spun to see her. "In two weeks."

"I'll be out of my sling by then."

"And?"

"I'd love to go."

Behind Libby, Charisse stomped her feet on the floor and rocked back and forth, celebrating his victory, and then she picked up her phone and began to text. Evan smiled. "Thank you, Libby. I can't wait."

Libby held up the folded square. "Thank you."

He walked outside, and his phone rang. The caller ID told him exactly who Charisse had texted. "Yes, Gideon?" he answered.

"Good boy. I told you it would work."

Evan clicked off the call. He raised his eyes to heaven. "Thank you, Lord. Thank you."

Libby opened the many folds of the paper as Charisse leaned forward. Libby ran her hand over it to clear out the creases. Her breath caught in her throat. "It's just as I imagined it could be."

"Didn't I tell you?" Charisse gushed. "Look at the fountain in front of the cottage."

"That's the office."

"Oh, no. I've seen the other designs he's drawn. This is only one of the many renderings he's prepared for you. Evan doesn't brag, but he's a wonderful architect. He picks and chooses his projects. The cottage might be an office, but your customers will believe they've stepped into a cozy little home. He also has another plan where he's designed a separate building for the customer flow and made this an actual cottage."

Evan was right. He'd brought her dream to life. Cobblestone paths wound their way through gardens and into a nursery area. The hot house was center stage with gardens meandering outside for customers to enjoy and to envision the plants in their own yards. The little white cottage with hunter-green shutters and a green roof sat at the front of the property.

Libby shook her head. "Why would he do all of this for me?"

"Libby, honey, why would he not?" Charisse smiled.

"I don't know," she said. "It's taken me so long to get used to the kindnesses of you and Gideon. I've never received so much in my life, and now this. I can't believe Evan would—"

"Oh, hi." Hope Astor plopped into the seat vacated by the elderly woman. "Libby? Libby? I'm sorry. I can't remember your name."

"Hope, enough." Hope's friend, Tiffany, stood behind the gorgeous blonde.

Charisse stood. "Let's go."

Libby motioned for Charisse to wait. "Hope, it's good to meet you again. Tiffany, good to see you." She folded the picture, but not before Hope's surprised gaze lifted from it to her. Hope probably recognized Evan's artistry.

"Hi," Tiffany said.

Libby stood and pushed her chair under the table. "My last name is Overstreet." She smiled. "But Libby is fine. I have to rush to an appointment, but I look forward to running into you again."

"I'm sure," Hope said, shaking her head as if Libby said something out of the ordinary. "Come on, Tiff. Let's get our coffee so we can head to the beach."

"By the way, *Hope*," Charisse waved her hand, "you sat in some spilled coffee."

"Charisse," Libby scolded in a whisper. "That wasn't nice."

"I know, but it sure felt good." Charisse pulled her out the door.

Evan studied the plans in front of him and looked back at his clients. "This change can't be made unless you're willing to spend a pretty penny. That's a bearing wall, not to mention the plumbing that will have to be moved. We'll need to file for new permits. Permitting will take a while, and I need to keep my crews working. So pending permits, I'll have them start some jobs that were ahead of yours, but once I have them start, I don't like to take them off a project before completion."

The husband puffed out his cheeks and ran his hand through his hair. "See, honey, nothing we can do."

"If you'd have allowed me to look at the plans in the first place, this wouldn't have happened, but no, you assumed I'd like it."

Evan took a deep breath, feeling for the man. He'd worked with the doctor and his wife for nearly six months, and the woman was never satisfied.

She peered down at Evan's plans. "I want this area open, a sweeping view from the kitchen into the family room and beyond to the gardens and the pool."

"Mrs. DeWinter ..."

The woman held up her hand, and Evan bit down hard on his tongue.

"No, Darla." Dr. DeWinter cut his wife off before she could speak again. "We're over budget. I have a girl in my office whose family is one paycheck away from the streets, and you're spending money on an ornate palace. I'm sorry. I'm drawing the line."

"Then I suppose we should stop the entire project. Or maybe you'll want to finish it and let the girl live there."

"That's not what I'm saying. We've worked with Mr. Carter to create a nice home, but Darla, nothing is ever good enough for you."

Evan's phone cut into the conversation. "Excuse me. I'll let you talk this over." He stepped out into the hall away from his conference room. "Evan Carter."

"Hi, Ev," Hope sang into the phone. "Look, we're over on the coast."

Evan slapped his hand against his forehead. He should have looked at the caller ID, but he'd been anxious to get out of the battle zone he'd lived in with the DeWinters since they hired him. "I'm working, Hope."

"But Tiffany and me, we've had a little too much to drink. We're over at Playalinda Beach."

Evan pressed his hand against the wall and leaned forward, his forehead resting on his arm. "Tiffany has a brother. Call Daniel."

"He's a doctor. He can't just leave his patients."

"And I'm with clients." He looked at his watch. "It's only two o'clock. Hang out there for a few hours and don't drink. When you're sober, drive home. That way you won't have to inconvenience someone else to drive you back for your car."

"Come on, Evan. You were never so practical before. What do you care about my car? I've left it places before. You never minded coming to rescue me, and we were never in a hurry to get the car back."

The truth. The princess wanted a hero to race to her side. "Hope, my white horse is out to pasture. I'm sorry."

And the reality was, he'd never been a hero.

"No, Ev. I think the truth is you want it to be in someone else's pasture, and you're pathetic. I'm thinking you need to take a drink so you can get the spot out of your eyes and see ugly when it's in your face." Her voice no longer sang with anticipation but dripped with slurred hatred, reminding him of Mrs. DeWinter. As far as Evan was concerned he—and Danny Duvall—had dodged a shrew-bullet.

Evan closed his eyes and ended the call. "Help them to get home safely, Lord." The prayer eased his conscience and took away the blaze of anger that burned inside of him. How had he ever managed to get in with that crowd?

His drinking. They said he was fun to be around as long as he had the right amount of liquor in his system, but tip the balance with a foul mood, and he could be an angry mess of trouble. In reality, he had thrived on the anger.

And with Hope's words about Libby, Evan was glad he wasn't drinking now. How could Hope think Libby ugly? She was the most beautiful woman on earth—inside and out.

Ugly was living a life with no appreciation of God's goodness.

"Mr. Carter." Dr. DeWinter opened the conference room door. His wife pushed past him and down the hall. "We may be putting it on the market as soon as it's built, but the plans will not change."

Evan nodded and shook the man's hand. "I'm sorry."

"Not your fault. I made the call, trying to take some of the pressure off of her, but she's a perfectionist, which may or may not break this marriage apart."

"Robert, I'm ready to go."

Dr. DeWinter shook his head in clear frustration.

"Now," his wife ordered.

"I'll be praying for you, Doctor." Evan shook the man's hand.

Ugly was having a wife who did not value you as the head of your household.

Evan thought of Libby, and the faith she'd placed in him and in Gideon to advise her about the nursery.

Yeah, Libby Overstreet was the most beautiful woman he'd ever met.

FAY LAMB

Chapter Seven

The Harry P. Leu Gardens held Evan spellbound, not because of their beauty, but because of Libby. He could walk beside her all day, enjoying the wonderment on her face. Like a small girl given a vast wonderland, Libby twirled one way and then another.

"Evan, look." She pointed to the rose garden ahead of them and then cupped her hands over her face, revealing only her wide green eyes through her new glasses. "They're lovely. Have you ever seen anything this beautiful?"

A couple walking in the opposite direction smiled at Evan and Libby as they passed. Each garden brought another level of amazement. He couldn't help but smile either as they meandered through the azalea garden encircling the two-hundred year old oaks, Spanish moss dangling from their branches.

She touched a leaf as if it was precious to her. "This reminds me of my grandmother's yard. Azaleas surrounded all her old oaks. Her yard came alive with pink and white blooms in late winter and early spring."

Libby would love his yard with its stately oaks and azaleas throughout the acreage. Maybe he should invite her over, cook dinner for her, steaks on the grill. They could dine by the lake.

He didn't want to push it. In the car, Libby seemed shy with him. If they could get by without a mishap, she might agree to dine with him tomorrow. Perhaps he would invite Gideon and Charisse to chaperone.

In the Home-Demonstration Garden, Libby examined the displayed architectural designs. "You're a wonderful architect, but you do more construction, don't you?" She gave him a sideways glance.

"I'm licensed, and I occasionally work a project from the plans up, but I'm more of a hands-on guy. I have a couple of architects in my office and two assistants, one's a bookkeeper, the other does the secretarial and permitting work for me, but I like to be a part of the actual building."

"Well, these ideas, they don't compare with what you designed for me."

"That wasn't an architectural plan. It was a rendering of what I think the property can become. When you purchase the place, we might have to modify some of the ideas if you liked them."

"But Charisse says she saw your plans for the buildings."

"When you sign the contract—"

"Still thinking about it." She flitted away from him.

"But Gideon said the owner has lowered the price to entice you." She was definitely avoiding the subject.

She studied another plan. "Most people believe women gossip. You and Gid put them to shame."

"Your rebuke is duly noted and recognized for the truth it is." He had to admit she was his favorite topic of gossip.

She smiled. "I was playing. Gideon trusts you. I knew that when I heard you ask him about V.J.'s adoption. They treat me like family. There isn't much about them I don't know. I assume Gideon has grown to think of you the same way."

"I hope he has." Because Gideon and Charisse had taken the place of his dysfunctional family. "So, you haven't accepted the offer?"

"When we first met, you said you were working on a personal project."

Now he was sure her avoidance was intentional. He let her have her way. Again, no need to push. "Yes, very personal. I'm building a small office overlooking the lake on my property. The plants I'm bartering with you will line the pathway between my house and the office."

They wandered through the different gardens and into the cemetery. Like him, she had a fascination for old gravestones. He thought of all the old graveyards throughout the United States they could visit, looking at history. "The original owners, the Mizells, are buried here," he told her. "Some of these date back to the 1860s. Imagine what living in Florida was like back then."

"My grandmother's grandmother lived here then." She did one of her little twirls toward him and then danced away, her interest settling on an older marker.

"Really?" He'd never known anyone with roots so deep in Florida history.

"My grandmother was born in Titusville in 1899,"

she said.

"A true Southern Belle, Ms. Libby. I'm delighted to know you, ma'am." He bowed.

She curtsied. "Maybe Southern, but surely no belle. My grandmother, though, was a bit of a Southern matriarch." They walked out of the cemetery and toward the Mizell-Leu house. Wide, open verandas jutted out from the first and second floor of the historic home. "Evan, can you imagine Harry and Mary Jane Leu living here, lovingly turning this property into what we see now only to leave it to the city so that others can enjoy the beauty? It's so romantic."

A vision of Libby working alongside him in the gardens of his home silenced him with awe.

"Is anything wrong?" Libby stopped.

He shook the pleasant imaginings from his mind and smiled. "No. I'm enjoying the sights." He wouldn't tell her he hadn't taken his eyes off her for an entire hour, watching her flutter from one plant to another, from one garden to the next. She chattered to him, sharing stories about her grandmother and her mother and about a great aunt who was a well-known horticulturalist in her day. Evan soaked in everything about her. He thought to ask her about her father, but he didn't want to intrude.

"Oh," she sighed. "Evan, you wanted to see the art exhibit. You've been so patient, and I've taken most of your day."

He'd rather see the smile on her face than any of the art displayed by local artisans. "We have time. Why don't we walk around the home? There's also a kitchen garden."

"I can tell this isn't your first trip here."

"No, when my mom was sick, she said she'd always wanted to visit. I wheeled her all over this place, enjoying it with her. The Enabling Garden was fun for her. She couldn't get out of her wheelchair, but the plants were at her level, and she could touch them and smell them." He wouldn't tell her how his mother had cried because bringing her here had been one of the very few joys she had in life. His happiness at spending time with his mother had been dampened by the knowledge that she didn't have long to live.

"My mother would have loved this place, too." Libby said.

"I think our mothers would have gotten along very well. They've both instilled in us a love for gardening."

Her lips curved upward into a smile.

He held out his hand and she took it, walking with him toward the home. "Evan." She turned the same look of wonderment to him as she'd shown during their odyssey in the gardens. "I've never had a better time in all my life. Thank you for inviting me."

He smiled. Neither had he.

Libby loved the feel of Evan's hand wrapped around hers. In the same way they studied the gardens, they now took their time looking at the exhibits, watercolors of

Florida's flora and fauna and wildlife. Sculptures of manatees, dolphins, pelicans, and other wildlife dotted the area. Oils depicted scenes of beauty found only in the swamps and the marshes of Florida, and in the faces of Floridians enjoying the unique landscapes of sea, rivers and, lakes.

"Oh." Libby reached toward a painting and then pulled her hand back, mesmerized by the likeness of the older woman with graying hair tied back in a bun. The lady stood sideways beside a gardenia bush. Her elderly face shone with love and tenderness as her wrinkled hand tilted a bloom downward toward a very young girl. The blonde-haired angel reached for it with a face filled with anticipation.

The detail was exquisite. The more she studied the painting the more acquainted she became with the lives depicted on the canvas. They stood in front of a 1950s style Florida home in a flower garden lining the front of the house. The older woman wore a dress with a broach pinned to the collar—not Victorian, but very much like a Southern woman who emerged into the 1960s and 1970s still a product of her past. The little girl's orange shorts and smock top were something similar to what Libby's mother had dressed her in as a small child.

"You like this?" Evan broke into her musings.

"I can't tell you how much. This has to be a picture from the artist's past. I'm reminded so much of my grandmother. My father's mother. Even after he abandoned my mother and me, my grandparents loved us so well."

Evan's tender hand brushed her hair from her face. "I'm so sorry that you still carry that pain."

She stared into his brown eyes. The tenderness she saw told her he meant every word.

She nodded and bit her lower lip to keep it from quivering before turning her attention back to the painting. She peered to see the signature of the artist.

Evan stepped in front of her. If she didn't know better, she'd think he was blocking her view. She shrugged. "It doesn't matter. The price is well worth it, but it's out of my range."

Evan slipped his arm around her shoulder and pulled her with him. "I like this one. What do you think?"

Her breath slowed. She concentrated on putting one foot in front of the other, Evan's touch keeping her from focusing on the art.

They turned the corner, and he pulled away from her. "Libby, I need to—you know." He pointed back in the direction of where they came. "Why don't you go on ahead, and I'll catch up to you."

Libby nodded. "Sure. I'll stay around here."

"Enjoy the art. I'll be right back." He backed away from her, and before she could tell him the restroom was in the other direction, he was out of sight.

She stayed in the general area where he could easily find her, but the picture of the woman and the girl called to her. Time passed, and Evan did not return. She began to worry he'd lost her. The gardens would close soon, and the crowd was thinning. Maybe something had caught his eye, and he'd stopped to browse.

One more look at the painting of the old woman and young girl would last her a lifetime. She walked back toward the aisle.

And her steps faltered.

Evan stood near the booth where she'd seen the painting. He was talking with a woman—a blonde. Libby could never mistake her beauty.

Hope Astor.

Evan leaned close to Hope. Libby wasn't sure, but she thought he'd just kissed his friend.

She watched for a moment. Hope looked in her direction and then blocked Libby's view of Evan.

Libby had been such a stupid, stupid fool. Why had he even asked her to come with him today?

He must have spotted Hope in the crowd, and he'd left Libby to see her.

She made her way through the crowd and outside into the evening heat. The botanical clock beckoned her with a promise that its beauty would stave away the devastating blow to her heart. She had to get her emotions under control. If Evan came looking for her, she wouldn't look like even more of a fool. If he went off with Hope, she'd just call a cab home.

But the thought of his abandonment squeezed her heart like the day so long ago when her father had walked out the door—a better life awaiting him—a life without her.

Chapter Eight

The crowd was thinning, and he'd been gone from Libby too long. Evan cast one last glance at the picture and looked back at its artist. "Hope, it's not sold."

Hope glared at him with icy blue eyes. "You didn't think I saw you. I watched her gawking at it. You're not buying my work for that little freak."

Evan clenched his fists and fought to control his temper. Libby was a freak only because Hope couldn't stand to look upon her goodness. She was everything Hope was not.

"You look liked a goof with your arm around that hideous creature."

"So, you're not going to sell me the painting?" He pulled back and looked one more time at the treasure he sought. All he could see was the enchantment on Libby's face as she took in the painting. He leaned toward her, his lips close to her ear. "What if I pay double what you're asking?"

She didn't need the money. She had all her mother and father's wealth. They'd spoiled her with it, teaching her that status and possessions were more important than the people who care for you and love you. The only reason Evan had made it into her crowd was her attraction for him, and her attraction was for a man fueled by alcohol, not the real him.

"Double?" She widened her eyes.

"Yeah, you heard me. Double."

Hope looked away from him but quickly turned back, moving closer. "I'll tell you what, Evan. Since you've made me look pathetic by hooking up with someone like that, you pay me three times my asking price, and it's hers. But I want to keep it here through the end of the exhibit tomorrow."

He dug in his pocket and pulled his debit card from his wallet. "Ring it up."

She stared at him for several moments. Her gaze rested on the picture. "You've got to be kidding me?"

"No, and a deal's a deal."

Obviously, she thought he wouldn't pay her price. Hope was wrong. He'd have paid anything she asked to see Libby's face when he gifted her with the painting.

Hope snatched the card from his hand, ran it through her system, and handed him the receipt to sign.

He scribbled his name. "And be sure to put a sold sign on it. I'll pick it up when you tell me."

"Will you answer me one question?" She stared at the receipt.

"If I can." He'd started away but stopped.

"Why her?"

"Because her beauty is genuine, Hope. I'm drawn to her like a magnet to steel." He jogged down to the end of the aisle and searched the crowd for Libby. He explored every corner of the exhibit without any luck. Outside the crowds were thinning. His gaze perused the gardens as far as he could see. There she was, by the botanical clock.

"Hey." He ran up to her. "I've been looking everywhere for you."

She didn't speak or turn. When he touched her shoulder, she tensed.

"Libby, I'm sorry. I didn't mean to be gone so long. I ran into someone."

She nodded. "They're closing soon."

"Are you okay?"

She turned. "I'm fine. I wanted to see the clock one more time. The flowers are so colorful."

He breathed a sigh of relief. She wasn't crying. Still, she was tense. He tugged at her sleeve. "Was I gone all that long?"

She tried to smile. Her lips twitched, but she didn't quite make it. Was she so insecure to think his absence meant he didn't find his time with her enjoyable? If he could only take her in his arms and assure her everything was fine.

No, he wasn't strong enough. His attraction would overpower his restraint. Like alcohol, she was a temptation, an invitation to open the door to past sins. If her desire for him was anything like his feelings, they could easily fall. The chance also existed that she didn't feel the same about him.

"We should go."

She stepped beside him, and they walked to his truck. He opened her door and offered his hand to help her up and inside. Once again, her body tensed under his touch.

Libby remained quiet as they drove back toward her apartment. "Would you like to get something to eat?" he asked.

"Not tonight, Evan. You've spent so much time with me today. I'm sure you're tired of my company."

"That will never be true. I enjoyed our time together, and I'd would love to go back. You can always draw from these gardens for ideas for your nursery."

She turned away from him, staring out the passenger window.

"Are you mad at me?"

She shook her head. "I'm tired. That's all."

They rode in silence. He pulled into her apartment complex and escorted her to the door. "Libby," he whispered her name. "Whatever I've done, I'm sorry."

She stuck the key in the lock and then faced him, her hand on the knob. "Evan, you are the nicest man I've ever met. The truth is, I haven't met very many. I'm sure as much as you and Gideon talk he's probably told you he thinks I'm sheltered. What he doesn't know is I haven't been sheltered enough, but still I'm not like your other friends."

"I don't understand." He brushed her hair with his hand.

Tears spilled over her green eyes. "I understand one date doesn't mean forever."

If she'd give him eternity, he'd marry her right now, on this very spot. He wouldn't care that he was capable of harming her.

He blinked. He had hurt her. The evidence was trailing down her beautiful face.

"I'm sorry, Evan. I can't do this."

Why did he feel those words all the way to the core of his being? The closing door slammed against his heart.

And he didn't even understand what he'd done.

Libby sat in the darkness of her room. Someone pounded on her front door.

"Libby, let me in, or I'll use my key," Charisse insisted. "I have it, and I won't hesitate."

"Use it already," Libby called from the hallway. She went into her bathroom and shut her door. Charisse needed to learn to stop meddling. The fact she was here said it all. Charisse and her husband had set this date up. Somehow, they'd convinced Evan to take her to the gardens.

She'd acted like a fool in front of him, flitting around the gardens, actually pretending that he wanted to be with her, and Evan was just nice enough to let her pretend.

But his attraction to Hope Astor was so very obvious. If seeing the painting one more time hadn't been so important, she'd still be blissfully ignorant. At least now, Evan was spared from ever needing to see Libby again. Still, he'd apparently cared enough to let Charisse know she was absolutely insane—breaking down and crying in front of him like a silly, lovesick, heartbroken fool.

Light filtered through the bottom of the bathroom door. "Where are you?" Charisse demanded.

Libby ran the water in the sink and splashed her face. "Are you okay?"

The faucet handle squeaked as she turned it off. With her eyes closed, she searched the counter for her towel and then patted her face. In the darkness, she couldn't see her image, but she'd bet her cheeks were red and splotchy from all the tears she'd cried.

"I'm waiting."

She wasn't going out until Charisse left. Libby backed up against the door and slid down. "I'm not coming out."

"Great. Just great. I came all the way over here to talk to a door."

"What made you think you needed to come over?" Libby slammed her fist against her leg.

"I'm here because a man who couldn't stand to be alone is sitting in my living room with my husband. He sought out Gideon rather than a bottle of whiskey."

"Nothing happened." Libby brought her knees up and lowered her forehead to them.

"He said you changed. You were as different as night and day. He can't figure out how he hurt you. I had to convince him you're not schizophrenic."

"Ha-ha. Not funny, Charisse." Libby banged her head against the door and placed her hand where it hurt.

"Libby, I gotta tell you something. You need to understand that Evan's being cautious with you because he's afraid of physically hurting you."

"That's ridiculous." She wiped her hands over her face.

"I shouldn't tell you this because Gideon shared it with me—"

"Don't gossip, Charisse."

"You need to know what you've done to the guy."

Libby opened her mouth wide in surprise. "What I did to him?"

"Libby, Evan has some deep scars—physical ones. Gideon says he was horribly abused by his father."

Evan had mentioned the abuse, but his main concern had been with the welfare of his brothers. She closed her eyes. If she was ever allowed to show him she loved him, she would show him how little the scars bothered her. She would caress them, and she'd love him so he could forget what Nate had done.

"In his mind, he's inherited his father's propensity toward aggression. He admits to being a violent drunk. So, when you became distant, and you didn't tell him what he'd done—"

"He left me in the middle of the art show, and he went back to find Hope Astor." In light of Charisse's words, it all seemed so childish to her now.

"Oops," Charisse said.

"Oops? Is that all you have to say?" Libby sat back. Her head thudded against the door again. She turned so she wouldn't repeat that mistake and then cried out at the ache in her unhealed shoulder.

"If I told you his meeting with Hope Astor was something you shouldn't have seen, what would you say?"

"What would I say?"

"Yeah, you weren't supposed to see them together."

"That's obvious," Libby agreed. "Are you telling me he told you he saw Hope? If so, why didn't he tell me? He must have known I was upset." She needed to let it go. Evan's heart was burdened because of her actions.

"Do you trust me?"

Libby thought for a minute. How could she say yes? Gideon and Charisse had brought Evan and her to this. "Not anymore."

"Yikes."

"Do you think I don't know you're behind this, you and Gideon? Look what you've done. Evan's hurting because of your meddling."

"Evan's ready to take a drink because he left you when you were upset, and he thinks he's the cause."

"Please tell him it has nothing to do with him." Really, it didn't. Evan was a victim of her traitorous, romanticizing heart. "Since you've shared his past with me, tell him I'm not ready for a relationship. I'm realizing I haven't gotten over the first rejection of my life."

"Libby, he's not rejecting you. Believe me. He had a very good reason for talking with Hope, and someday you'll understand. I just can't tell you right now."

Libby stood. "I'm not good enough for him. Evan needs someone like Hope Astor. She's sophisticated, beautiful, and not as childish as me."

"I'm sorry, Libby, but you think that—that trollop—is sophisticated and beautiful? And mature? Hope Astor has a lot of growing up before she'll ever have what you have. And while I'll agree you're being a little immature about this, I understand. Evan is your first real love. But, honey, you don't know the hold you have over people who are lucky enough to get to know you."

Libby opened the door. "Some hold I have over him, huh? He's sitting at your house so he won't drink. If you and Gideon had stayed out of this, Evan would never have met me. He'd be fine, and so would I."

"And you'd both be miserable trying to figure out how to say hello to one another. You are so transparent. I watched you the first time you saw him. Libby, your eyes took on a twinkle I haven't seen in forever—not since we were kids."

Libby stared at Charisse. Was her friend a lunatic? "Do I look happy now?"

"You are. You're living in incredible blissfulness. You just don't know it yet." Charisse turned on her heels.

"Where are you going?"

"I'm going back home to tell Evan what's got you so upset—let the air out of his balloon of despair."

Libby started to speak, but Charisse sprang out her door. Libby sank to the floor in disbelief. If this was happiness, she'd rather return to the sad, lonely, pathetic life she had a year before. At least her mother never spoke in riddles.

Chapter Nine

Another morning and Libby was absent from Java Lava. Delilah and Hope sat in the back deep in conversation. Evan purchased his morning cup of coffee and escaped unnoticed.

He wanted as little confrontation as possible with Hope. The exhibit ended the day after he'd purchased the painting for Libby. Weeks passed and Hope still refused to hand him the gift, always offering an excuse.

Libby, he'd learned through Gideon, had forfeited her escrow on Nardone's Nursery. She'd just thrown her dreams away, and Evan still had trouble understanding why, even though he had no intention of allowing her to toss them aside so easily. A smile tipped his lips when he thought of the new project his crew was undertaking. They'd start the work today.

He lumbered down the sidewalk toward his downtown office. Once, he'd looked forward to designing and building a small space on his property where he could work in the early morning or late evenings, but he now lived for any chance to see Libby at Java Lava.

He passed Margie's Floral Arts. Flowers? Why hadn't he thought of that? He could send a bouquet to Libby with a note. Charisse had told him Libby had misunderstood his meeting with Hope at the gardens, and he still wanted to surprise Libby with the painting. Until Hope gave it to him, he didn't want to tell Libby about his surprise. Maybe flowers would tip the scales of Libby's forgiveness in his favor and allow him to come into the beauty of her presence.

Before he entered the shop, he saw her. He peered through the door at the one person who hadn't left his thoughts in days. As if steel lined his heart and she was the magnet drawing him to her, he pushed open the door. A tinkling bell announced his arrival.

The place smelled of damp soil, a symbol of budding life. Jasmine and lavender wafted through the air, scents of calm and tranquility. He drank in the aroma and delighted in the sight of his earth-bound angel.

Libby looked up from pricing the potted Geraniums. She gazed at him from behind those smaller glasses he wished she'd change. He missed the pair his father had busted.

"It is you." He touched the leaf on a plant near the door.

Libby scribbled on a small white square. "Yes." She dropped the tab and pushed a makeshift cart toward him.

"How long have you worked here?"

She started to write on another tab but allowed it to fall, giving him her full attention—exactly what he longed to have. "Not long. I was hired the day before I got injured."

He shook his head, hoping to stop her from any further mention of the nightmarish event. Did a disaster have to occur with each of their meetings? What could happen this time? Would a shelf of plants fall on her? Would one of the many chimes hanging from the ceiling clang down upon her head? "Libby, I owe you an apology. Charisse told me why you were upset with me. I should have called, but I felt you would rather I stay away."

That and with Hope holding the painting hostage, he had nothing to offer Libby as proof of the reason he'd sought out his old friend.

"After what Nate did to you, what I've done to you, I don't blame you for never wanting to see me again." Carefully planned words, ones he'd rehearsed in his head for days. An attempt to get her to say anything to encourage him in his pursuit of her.

"Nate isn't responsible for his actions, Evan. You must know that." She ran her fingers through the waves of her thick mahogany-colored hair.

He wished he could touch the strands, feel their silkiness. They were as soft as her tender soul.

"I don't blame Nate, and I don't blame you. Neither of you are responsible for this. Nate didn't know what he was doing, but Gideon and Charisse have pushed us together time and time again."

He wouldn't go there with her. Someone as innocent as Libby would never understand the evil Nate posed to everyone who crossed his path. He'd learned through Scripture that when you have nothing good to say about someone, you should keep your mouth shut, so he nodded. After all, honoring one's parent could be done with silence as well as praise. As for himself, he had no defense. He was his father's son. No matter that she'd misunderstood his meeting with Hope. He'd gone about meeting Hope in the wrong way. All he'd thought of was getting the desire of Libby's heart, and instead he'd crushed her. "Gideon and Charisse love you. Don't let me come between you, please."

"How is he? Your dad. I haven't been able to see him." She picked up another tag.

"I've asked that I be his only visitor."

"I know."

Of course Libby would know. Didn't she understand it was for her safety? She probably tried to see him again. He suspected she wanted to apologize to Nate—for what Nate had done to her.

"Do you?" she asked.

"Do I what?" Evan released the leaf he barely remembered touching.

"Do you visit with your father?" She speared him with her beautiful green-eyed gaze.

"Not as much as I did before he attacked you. I cause the anger in him to flare."

Libby shook her head. "I'm sorry, Evan, for your loss." She started away from him once again pushing the cart and placing items on the shelf.

"Nate Carter is no great loss to me." So much for honoring the old man.

Libby looked up once again. "And I'm sorry for that as well."

Evan could only nod. Her voice held a tone of

dismissal. He started for the door but turned. "May I ask you something?"

Her fingers turned white against her grip on the handle of the cart, but she nodded.

"You said you took this job before my dad hurt you."

"Yes. The owner held the position open for me until I got a doctor's okay to work."

"So when we were at the gardens and you came alive, walking among the flowers and the trees, when you held out your hands in the butterfly garden to let them come to you—you already knew you weren't going to buy the nursery?"

She didn't answer.

"You let Gideon think you might still do it. You made me believe I was helping you to understand dreams can come true?"

"My dreams don't come true, Evan. They never have."

"Because you let them go so easily."

Sadness crept over her beautiful face like a lurking shadow. She released her grip on the handle and turned back to marking the tags. "There are two kinds of fairy tales. Not all of them are the happily-ever-after kind. I learned a long time ago my life is the type that never has a happy ending."

"And for that, Libby, I'm sorry." He pulled the door open and walked outside. Watching her through the glass, he saw her shoulders tremor. She covered her face with her hands.

No shelf of plants had fallen on her. The chimes still hung from the ceiling, but Evan could see the disaster of this meeting as well. A tender flower crushed by life lay before him, and his clumsily asked questions had caused her to wilt.

Libby pulled her car alongside the gate leading onto the property she'd once envisioned as her business. Nothing had changed since the day they'd looked it over and determined she could handle the repairs and the workload. It hadn't been all that long ago, yet an eternity had crept away.

She wanted to walk the grounds, to talk to God, to give her dreams over to Him, hoping God, despite her irrational behavior, might again give her the okay to purchase the property.

A truck parked in the drive hindered her plans. A contractor's truck.

Someone must have purchased the nursery. Overwhelming disappointment threatened to overtake her as she pulled the folded piece of paper from her purse. She straightened it over her steering wheel. Her trembling fingers traced the line of the small cottage and meandered down the cobblestoned path Evan had depicted.

She looked out her window to the piece of property. She'd seen the potential; so had Evan. She cupped her hand over her lips and fought against the sobs welling up inside her.

She bowed her head and took a steadying breath. She needed to stop feeling sorry for herself, especially since this was all her doing. "Lord, I pray You bless the new owners; make them to thrive in business and in happiness. Dear Father, make all their dreams comes true, and forgive my heart's disappointment, Lord. I know You have better plans for me." She wiped the tears away.

Seeing Evan in the flower shop squashed any self-esteem she had garnered from her new employment. The rift she'd caused between father and son made it near impossible to face him. The nurses said Nate occasionally remembered her, and she left little gifts for him: a tract, a card, something that would allow her to share the love of God with a man who needed God's embrace. The aides provided Libby with the grim prognosis. If Nate continued as he was, very soon he would slip away into a world of utter confusion that would leave him unable to function at all.

She'd asked the head nurse only the night before if her pastor could visit Evan's father. They'd indicated that under the circumstances, Libby needed permission from Evan. Surely, he had asked his pastor to give his father some comfort. She could ask Charisse, but she didn't want to interfere any more than she had in Evan's affairs. Instead, she would pray for Nate and continue to keep a safe distance between Evan and her.

Charisse had been right. She'd acted like a child. First, her silly daydreams had made Evan into the perfect man, the one she could love for the rest of her life. If that wasn't bad enough, when he gave another woman his attention, her insides collapsed like a loaf of bread under a bag of groceries.

How had Evan taken hold of her heart so quickly? She prayed daily for the Lord to relieve her of the thoughts she held for him. The remembrance of his arm around her still quickened her pulse, and one look at him made her weak with loneliness. As at other times when she thought of him, the doubts didn't lag far behind. Evan was a handsome, successful man. Handsome and successful men didn't fall at Libby Overstreet's awkward, inept feet. They ran from her—even when she was a child.

"Ma'am, can I help you?"

She hadn't noticed the man approaching her car, and he startled her. "No. No. I'm sorry." She folded Evan's rendering quickly and tucked it in her purse. "I just wanted to look at the place."

"The new owner closed on the property last week. That's why we're here." The man stepped to the gate. He stuck his hand through the open window of her car. "I'm Charlie."

She shook his hand. "Libby Overstreet." She hoped the turn of her lips resembled a smile.

"I'm estimating the cost of some of the repairs and remodeling for the guy, though I suspect he already knows."

Libby nodded. "Tell him he bought a great place. Someone looked at it for me recently and told me I couldn't go wrong."

"Any reason you didn't purchase it?"

"Nothing to do with the property." She swallowed down the truth. "Well, Charlie, it's nice to meet you."

"Nice to meet you, too, ma'am."

Sitting in the oversized chair in Charisse's home, Libby rocked back and forth as she cried.

Charisse sat on the ottoman in front of the chair. Gideon came into the room and handed something to his wife before making a speedy escape.

"Libby, breathe." Charisse handed Libby a damp washcloth, and Libby wiped her eyes and her red nose.

"I wanted it so bad."

"But, honey, the nursery was yours for the taking. You could have owned it weeks ago, and you walked away."

"Evan."

"Evan, Evan, Evan." Charisse placed her hands on her hips, staring at Libby and shaking her head. "You could have owned the place and never looked at him again. What a silly reason to let go of your dreams so easily."

Evan's words, spoken to her in the florist shop. Both Charisse and Evan were correct. She'd allowed her past to dictate her actions. She'd given up on her dream of owning a nursery much too effortlessly. If her dreams never came true, maybe she was the cause. But it was too late now.

Libby hiccupped and stood from her chair. "I know you're right, but from the moment Gideon introduced me to Evan, he became part of the dream. I wanted him and the nursery or nothing."

"Liberty Overstreet, that's rash and irresponsible thinking. A man doesn't make your destiny."

"Oh, you can say that. You wanted law school and a husband. You got them both." The words flew from her without so much as a careful thought.

Charisse didn't answer, and Libby's eyes filled with fresh tears. Her jealousy had reared its ugly head and made her speak out of turn. She had once again hurt her friend because of her feelings for Evan.

She plopped back down into her seat. "No, Charisse. You lost law school after you lost Vance. You gained law school after God gave you Gideon. I'm happy for you. I'm just feeling sorry for myself. I never thought I could hurt you once, but now I've done it twice. And you're only giving me the truth. I thank you for loving me enough to tell me when I'm being foolish, which lately has happened a lot."

Charisse pulled Libby into a tight embrace. "Love causes us to do some pretty stupid things. You're not immune, Libby Overstreet."

"That's just it. I've never had any man treat me the way Evan did even if only for a short while." She clung to her old friend. "When he put his arm around me or when he held my hand, I lost all reason. My heart pounded, 'He's the one,' and with every beat, it still continues the chant. I pray to God to lessen the misery. I busy myself with work and ministry. I tell myself someone like me doesn't interest a man like Evan, but Charisse, desire still burns so hot, and I can't dampen the fire."

Charisse pulled away from her and held her with a steadfast gaze. "Tell that to Evan. If someone said they loved me like that, I'd melt in his arms."

For the first time Libby almost smiled. "Yeah, I watched you do it when Gideon proposed."

"Proposed? The man read me an edict. Don't change the subject. You know it works. You saw it work in my life. Go for it."

Libby shook her head. "I couldn't stand his rejection."

"You're not doing too well without one either. A rejection would at least give you closure."

"Charisse, you know what happened. My dad rejected me. Five years old and tears streaming down my face, asking him to love me, and he turned and walked out our door. If rejection brings closure, I must have missed something."

"Personally, I think the boy loves you as much as you love him, and you're both miserable because of it."

A few weeks earlier, Charisse declared Libby was happy and didn't know it. Now, she'd obviously changed her mind or come to her senses. Libby would never understand this love business. She didn't know if she wanted to.

Libby held the wet cloth against her face. "Evan

could never love me."

"Yeah, I believe that."

With a slow, weary movement, Libby looked to her friend. Was this retribution for her earlier remark about law school?

Charisse winked. "Evan has proved himself to me, Liberty Overstreet. He's too much of a gentleman to intrude on a woman who runs from him at every opportunity. Give him a chance."

Libby shook her head. "I can't stand the pain of knowing the truth of what he thinks of me."

Charisse raised her hands to the heavens and then pressed them against Libby's cheeks. "Your father lost out on an opportunity to know a wonderful young lady. I hope you'll reconsider and allow Evan the opportunity your father never took."

Libby shook her head. She'd never told Charisse the entire ugly story of her father's rejection. Her father hadn't missed out on an opportunity. He'd run from it. Charisse had no way of knowing what she asked of her.

Chapter Ten

Libby turned the page of her Bible and looked once more to the door. How could she both want to see someone so badly and dread his appearance at the same time?

"Here you go, Libby, coffee with cream and sugar." Charisse worked her way through the early-morning crowd gathered at Java Lava. Libby looked up from her Bible and pulled out the chair beside her.

Charisse sat. "I don't know what's keeping Delilah this morning."

Charisse had suggested meeting here for daily morning devotionals. Delilah loved the idea enough to get up early. Libby was always up early, and despite her fear of running into Evan, she had agreed. So far, Evan had not been in for his usual cup of coffee—not that Libby didn't look up each time the door opened.

"Here she comes." Charisse pointed.

"Sorry, I'm late." Delilah's purse reached her chair before she did. "I ran into some friends, and I asked them to join us. I hope you don't mind."

Libby offered Charisse a knowing look. Since when did Delilah care who joined them?

"Of course not," Charisse said.

"Delilah," a woman called from the front of the shop.

"Uh-oh," Charisse murmured. "Not good."

Libby cast a glance in that direction. The smile she planned to greet the newcomers with vanished like the drawing on a shaken Sketch-a-Doodle. "Hope." Determined not to act as foolishly as she'd done in the past, Libby pushed a new smile into place.

Hope narrowed her eyes and snapped her fingers. "I remember you. Libby, right? But I don't remember your last name. Oh, that's right. Evan couldn't recall it either, could he?" She laughed so loudly two ladies at the next table turned to stare.

Charisse stood. "That's a tired old joke, and if you use it again, I'll—"

"Hi." Hope's friend Tiffany advanced on the table. She held out her hand. "Libby, Charisse." Her heavy ponytail bounced with her personality. "I was looking forward to meeting you two again. Delilah has told me so much about you."

Libby shook the girl's hand. "I'm glad to see you, too."

"Tiffany, it is nice to meet you, but excuse us, Delilah." Charisse picked up her coffee and her Bible and motioned for Libby to join her. "We'll sit over there." She pointed to a table across the room. "You visit with your friends, and if we have time for our devotional, we'll take it."

"Charisse, please. Sit down." Libby reached for Charisse's arm. "Hope's probably as bad at remembering names as I am." She held out her hand toward Hope.

The woman didn't move for a second, but then she reached forward and shook Libby's outstretched hand with minimal effort.

"Glad that's over." Delilah motioned to a counter clerk. "Three coffees, black."

"Delilah." Libby shook her head.

Unlike everyone else in the coffee shop, Delilah insisted her coffee be served. Would she ever get used to Delilah's brashness?

"How do you know each other so well?" Hope asked. "I mean, you don't actually run in the same circles, do you?"

Delilah faced Hope. "We're sisters."

"Delilah, I've known you most of our lives. You're an only child," Hope argued.

"Not any longer. My Father has many children, and these two are my closest siblings."

Libby leaned forward. "What Delilah is telling you is that we share the same Father—our heavenly Father."

Hope started to take her coffee from the waitress, and if the girl had released her hold, the black liquid would have spilled onto the floor. "Not you, too. This Jesus stuff has got to end. It's bad enough when a Little Mary Sunshine like Libby here, who needs to cling to some kind of false hope, starts believing these fables, but you, Delilah. I thought you had brains."

Libby watched Delilah for an uncomfortable moment. Would the Scriptures they'd shared over the last few months sustain her under the ridicule of her friend?

Tiffany leaned in as if waiting to hear what Delilah would say.

Delilah took the coffees from the girl who still held them, her attention obviously riveted on the conflict unfolding in front of her. "Thanks," she said, and Libby shared a smile with Charisse. This time, Delilah's common courtesy—something they'd been working on—came without thought. A major victory since Delilah used her brashness as a hedge of protection against perceived slights.

Delilah motioned for Hope to sit, and when her friend refused, Delilah remained standing. "I've lived the life you're living, Hope, and I've discovered that my friend, Little Mary Sunshine, is living the reality. The bars, the men, the fast life, those fairy tales don't end in happily ever after. The prince of this world doesn't ride a shiny white horse, and he doesn't save us from the evil trolls or climb up a high tower to rescue us from our captor. He's the one who enslaves, and we don't even see our prison while we're living in it."

Libby lowered her head. She'd told Evan her fairy tales weren't the happily-ever-after kind. How had she forgotten God was in control, and no matter what happened on this earth, her forever after would be a joyous eternity?

"... so step out of the world and join us on the fun side of life. I've never been happier," Delilah finished whatever she'd been saying. Libby gave silent praise to God who had given Delilah the wisdom to use Hope's fairy-tale argument to witness to her friend and speak wisdom into Libby's heart. Delilah's brashness did have a place after all.

"Excuse me while I vomit." Hope turned on her heels. "Come on, Tiff. We'll see you when you float back to earth, Dee."

Delilah started after Hope, but Libby stopped her. Hope's friend seemed torn about whether to stay or to go. "Tiffany, please stay. Have a seat." Libby touched the woman's arm and smiled at Delilah. "Give me a second." She moved past her friend. "Hope?"

The woman turned. Her stern blue eyes held Libby in abeyance. "I don't want to hear about Jesus Christ." Her hoarse, hateful whisper almost broke with emotion. "Get away from me."

Libby reached in her purse and pulled out a handmade business card. "If you ever want to talk about anything, please call me."

Hope reached for the card but withdrew her hand. "I won't need to call you."

"Maybe you won't, but if you do, people tell me I'm a good listener." Libby never moved her hand.

Hope snatched the card from her and hurried out of the coffee shop.

A light touch on her arm brought Libby's gaze upward and into Evan's brown eyes.

"Evan." She breathed his name. God was giving her the chance to apologize to him and to explain that she did have a happily-ever-after. She'd been looking for it in the wrong place. "I'm so glad you're here. Delilah and I were talking with Hope."

He took a deep breath and let it out with the shake of his head. "Please leave Hope alone, Libby."

Libby bit her tongue, holding her gasp at bay.

"Can we talk?" he asked.

He'd already said enough. His feelings were evidently clear, and she wouldn't bother him again "I understand, and there's no reason to say anything." She stepped away from him.

"Libby, I can't—you have to know—"

"Please don't say anything." She held up her hand.

"What are you so afraid of?" He touched her shoulder.

"For heaven's sake, why would I be afraid of you?" She pushed open the door.

She'd lied. Libby was frightened to death of him and what his verbal rejection would do to her heart. She wouldn't stand in the way of his happiness, but she wouldn't let him say the words that she might never recover from. "Good-bye, Evan," she said the words, and they cut deeply into her heart.

Evan lifted the hard hat from his head and wiped the sweat away. How would he ever vanquish the memory of the look in Libby's eyes this morning and her response to his unfinished declaration of love? *For heaven's sake, why would I be afraid of you?* Evan had not mentioned any fear she might have for him, but her very question told Evan she was frightened of him, of what she experienced in Nate that very well could be a part of his makeup.

Stepping through the door of the building and out into the bright sunlight, Evan shielded his eyes with his hand. The grounds were coming along as he had designed, and the buildings on the property were taking on the ambience he had intended.

A review of the project caused the first smile in over a month to play at the corner of his lips. "You like?" One of the landscapers walked passed him. Evan did not recognize him. His own crew had learned lately to give him a wide berth. The subcontractors would probably learn sooner or later.

Evan did like what he saw. He'd prayed over the project every step of the way, including the purchase of the property. God's love toward him gave warmth to an otherwise dreary existence. The Lord's provision had been boundless, but at the same time, Evan felt like a small boy given only half of the prize he coveted.

His anger with Nate had not abated, and Evan discovered, he no longer craved the adrenaline that came with that emotion. All types of feelings filled him now: love, wonder, peace, anticipation, joy, guilt and heartache. They swirled about him. Apparently that dark hole in his soul had been a large one because there was enough inside him to run the gamut of emotions.

He'd visited his father on a few occasions and only when the guilt could not be overridden. Evan had agreed with the doctor's recommendations. To protect the lives of the nursing staff and the occupants of the nursing home, Nate needed to remain in a secure room. Why, then, did he feel so remorseful about the decision?

The smile disappeared. A member of his crew started to speak to him but walked away.

"What is it, Charlie?"

Charlie doubled back. "The place has a plumbing problem we didn't anticipate, Evan."

Evan frowned. "What's the deal?"

"Got a pipe or two busted under the cottage's foundation. It'll raise the cost of this work by about 10K if we do the job right."

"When have you ever seen me do a job wrong?"

"You know what I meant. I don't know what's gotten into you lately."

"Show me the problem." Evan pushed past him. "And stay out of my business."

Charlie muttered as he followed behind Evan, and Evan did not challenge him. Charlie was his right-hand man. He owned his own construction company, and when business was light, he worked with Evan, part of Evan's crack construction crew, and his go-to person when he acted as architect on this project. Charlie knew how to get the job done right the first time.

For I have given you an example, that you should do as I have done.

The Scripture he'd read in his morning devotional sprang from deep inside of Evan, reminding him his bad mood was not an example of Christ, and Charlie needed Christ.

As they stepped into the cottage, Evan stopped. "Charlie, I owe you an apology."

"Don't worry about it."

"I'm walking around acting like a madman, and no one on this crew deserves it. Everyone is working hard, and they're taking pride in a job well done."

"Love can make a normal man crazy." Charlie rubbed his bald head and smiled. "When I met my wife, I was miserable for a year until I finally got a ring on her finger and made her mine. Drove me insane thinking someone could take her away from me."

"I'm not in love," Evan denied.

"Yeah, sure, hoss. Whatever you say, but I know the symptoms, and I think you're a goner for sure."

There was no fooling that guy. Evan shook his head. "Show me the plumbing, Cupid."

Charlie led the way to the bathroom at the back of the house. Evan saw the problem and stood for a long time. He had options and just needed to make the right decision. Charlie waited in silence.

"Not a bearing wall?" Evan knew it wasn't but gave Charlie the respect he deserved by asking.

"Nope."

"The flooring and this wall have to be torn out." Evan walked from the bathroom toward the area where he planned to install a small kitchen. Again, he studied the situation before speaking. "Since we have to tear up the foundation, I think I can make a nice change here. I'll have a plan drawn up tomorrow. It'll fall within the scope of the permit. No problem there."

"Are you thinking what I think you're thinking? Hoss, that'll cost an arm and a leg. Does your client have the money? I've never known you to replace when it can be refurbished."

"This project must have perfection written all over it, Charlie. I'm the client, and I'll pay whatever it takes to get it done correctly."

"Yes, sir."

"Do you know if my office ordered the granite mantel for the fireplace?"

"You're the client?" Charlie questioned. "And you're putting that much money into a fireplace mantel for a business?"

"Yeah, I hope to have something pretty special hanging over it. I need the right color, the right size, and that's the price I had to pay."

"For perfection." Charlie nodded. "Yeah, you're a goner. That's for sure. I hope the woman you're doing this for is worth it."

"She's more valuable than rubies, Charlie. Much more valuable." Evan slapped the older man on the shoulder. "Thanks for your concern. I appreciate it when a crew member wants to save me money."

"Love makes us do all kinds of crazy things." Charlie winked.

"Yes, Charlie, it does. I'd do anything to make this pain go away."

Libby

"Marry her, Ev. That's all I got to say."

"I wish it were that easy." If it were, he'd have married her the first day he met her, without thought, without reason, without prayer. His dream-come-true, though, would be her living nightmare.

Chapter Eleven

Libby would never forgive Charisse. When she'd arrived for dinner at the Tabors' home, Gideon introduced another guest, an intern with Gideon's office. A major setup.

She'd met Scott once before, a brief exchange. He was handsome enough, but his arrogance impeded his good looks, at least as far as Libby was concerned. Still, he didn't deserve this.

Gideon and Charisse excused themselves to the kitchen. Libby leaned toward Scott, placing her hand on his expensive suit sleeve. "I'm so sorry."

Scott shrugged and pulled his arm away. He gave a nervous glance toward the kitchen but said nothing. With his validation of her thoughts, he might as well have slapped her.

The man obviously found nothing attractive about her. Just how had Evan managed to take her out in public and spend the entire day with her?

Her napkin fell from her lap, and she bent to retrieve it.

The doorbell rang, and Libby peered out the picture window to the front stoop.

Evan.

Gideon hurried past the dining room to answer the

door.

And all at once, the plan her matchmaking friends had devised fell into place.

Libby sprang upward, knocking over her chair. She tried to recover, but her body slammed against the table, rattling the dishes. A water goblet wobbled and tipped over. Libby held the napkin over her face as the water spilled onto Scott's lap.

He jumped to his feet. His plate caught in his napkin and flew into the air, its contents splattering across his chest.

Scott gave an angry brush at the food. "Look what you've done? You idiot."

Libby stepped back. Her napkin slipped from her grasp at his heart-wrenching words.

Evan and Gibeon entered the dining room as Libby turned from the table. She gasped when her gaze collided with Evan's.

His jaw clenched as he moved forward, stepping around Scott's chair. Evan raised his fist. "What did you say to her?" He stood in front of her, blocking her view of Scott. "What did you call her?"

"This suit cost me a fortune."

"I think your money would have been better spent on a course in manners." Charisse made her presence and her displeasure with her dinner guest known.

Evan gripped Scott's collar and turned the man to face Libby. "Apologize to the lady," he demanded, his fist still raised.

"Maybe she should apologize to me with a check for

the dry cleaning."

"I'll write your check," Gideon spoke for the first time. "But right now, I think you need to do as my friend says."

"She did this to me." Scott jerked from Evan's hold, threw the napkin on the table, and stomped toward the door.

"Hey," Evan caught him by the shoulder.

Scott turned.

Evan's fist moved through the air, aimed at Scott's face.

"Evan!" Libby covered her face with her hands and peeked through her fingers.

"Whoa." Gideon's quick action snatched Evan's arm, stopping the swing midway to its target. He jerked Evan back, pinning his arms. Gideon nodded to Scott. "I think you better leave before I let him have you. And you better take this evening to determine if you can treat others with more respect than you've treated members of my family. If not, I'll notify the school you won't be returning to my office to finish your internship."

"Gideon," Libby whispered. "This isn't Scott's fault. You placed him *and Evan* in this position."

Scott had walked toward the door, but he stopped. His gaze fell on her. "This wasn't your idea?"

Evan watched her as he strained against Gideon's hold.

"No, Scott. I have never asked my friends to set me up on a date. They're good enough at meddling all on their own."

Scott's jaw clenched then released. "I overreacted. I thought you'd asked them to invite me, and I felt obligated." He glared at Gideon.

Libby squared her shoulders. "I would never do anything like that." She took a deep breath. "And if I did, I'd want someone with more character, a man who wouldn't so blatantly point out all of my flaws." She caught the hint of a smile on Evan's face. What had she just said? "Scott, I'm—"

"Don't you dare apologize to him." Charisse shook her head. "Little Libby has her day." Her friend wrapped her in a hug.

Scott left without another word.

Evan struggled for release from Gideon's hold.

"Can I trust you if I let you go?" Gideon loosened his grasp but still held to his friend.

Evan didn't answer.

Gideon turned Evan toward her.

Evan winced when he looked at her, whether from pain or her not-so-pretty face, Libby didn't know.

"Now, can I trust you?" Gideon repeated.

Running out the door was not an option as Scott had just exited, and she never wanted to see him again.

"Answer me." Gideon kept his voice low and controlled. Libby had never seen him so irate. But Gideon and Charisse were to blame. She was as sure of it as she was of Scott's lack of manners.

Evan nodded.

Released, Evan reached for her.

She backed away from him. "I need to go. I'll get my purse." She moved around the far side of the table.

"Libby, I'm sorry. He seemed like such a nice man." Charisse followed her into the living room.

"He's not Evan," Libby whispered. "You should have known. No one else will do. No one but Evan."

"Then for goodness' sakes, tell him. He's right here."

Libby grabbed her purse and swung around toward her friend. "I told you. Rejection hurts, Charisse. I know you can't understand, but I ache with it. Please don't do this again. I'll forgive you this once, but the Lord will have to take me to task before I forgive you a second time."

"Libby, that didn't look like rejection to me. He protected your honor."

"But Scott is right. I am an idiot. Evan just has more tact and a different way of saying what he's thinking."

"How do you know what he's thinking? You won't even give him the chance." Charisse stomped her foot like an immature teenager.

"I don't want to hear him say it. If he told me the truth—Charisse, if he told me the truth the way Scott did—I'd curl up and die."

"Scott is the idiot. But what if Evan said what you want to hear?"

Libby tried for a moment to push past Charisse but her resolve wilted. "I can't take that chance. I never told you the entire story about my father. Do you know what my earliest childhood memory is? I recall it as vividly as if it were yesterday. My fifth birthday. My mother and father. She stood behind me while I sat on a stool in front of the table where my birthday cake had five candles glowing. My father stood across the small table in front of me. They were arguing. Mom asked him not to ruin my birthday. He took a swing at my mother, and he hit me instead. I fell off the stool onto the terrazzo floor. I hit my head and the breath was knocked out of me. My mother bent over to help me. I started to cry for him. I lifted my hands, wanting him to pick me up and say he was sorry. Instead my dad pointed at me and said, *'That* is the cause of all our problems.'" Libby covered her heart with her hands. Had she really told Charisse the story no one but her mother *and her father* knew about? "My own dad hated me."

Charisse's face lost its color. She seemed to sway, but she recovered. "I always thought that your dad and mine had just left us. I—I don't know what to say. I'm so sorry he hurt you that way."

"I couldn't stand Evan's dismissal of me. Don't you see? I had my mother to lean on back then. Now, I have— I have no one."

Charisse folded Libby in her arms. "You have your heavenly Father. God loves you and so do we. You also have Delilah. If you haven't realized it yet, we all feel like we're your family."

Her friend was right. God was her Father, not some selfish, cruel man from long ago, and though she'd lost her mother, God had replaced that love three-fold. "You're right, and I'm being silly."

"Libby?" Evan came from behind them.

Libby pulled away from Charisse.

"I'm sorry if I upset you." Evan stood before her like an apologetic child. Gideon loomed behind him reminding Libby of an enforcer. "My temper—as you can see and as I've told you—I have a problem with it sometimes."

If she stayed, Evan could destroy the little bit of self-esteem she had left. "I have to go." She pushed past him.

Evan reached out and grasped her arm. "Don't. Not because of me."

Libby jerked from his grip. Her purse spilled across the foyer. The contents rolled in every direction and under each piece of furniture. She took a deep breath as the others scrambled to help her.

When they gathered everything, Evan held out her purse, fully packed and in complete disarray. "Stay. Enjoy your evening. I'll leave."

"I have to get home," Libby lied. She had no one at home who needed her.

She turned away from them. All she wanted was to be needed—and desired. She took a trembling breath … to be *cherished.*

"May I drive you?" Evan asked.

"I have my car. Thank you, though."

"Libby." Gideon touched her shoulder. "You're obviously a little upset. Why don't you let Evan take you in your car? Charisse and I can drive our car and bring Evan back."

"No, that's okay."

"Give me the honor," Evan pleaded. "You shouldn't drive now."

Trapped. Ride all the way to her house with Gideon and Charisse fawning over her like a child or drive with Evan, hearing him close the door on her foolish dreams. "I guess I have no choice."

If Libby sat any further from him, she'd be traveling on the outside of her small sedan. Neither spoke as the lights of Orlando passed them by. They rolled up to a tollbooth, and Evan reached in his pocket for the money required to take the expressway to Libby's apartment. The booth attendant smiled at him. "You and your wife have a lovely evening."

Evan looked to Libby who appeared horrified at the thought of being his wife. He simply thanked the man and rolled up the window. "Libby." He looked over at her. "Again, I'm sorry."

"You were very nice to come to my rescue, Evan, but I'm glad Gideon didn't let you punch Scott."

"I am, too. I flew off the handle. I wish I could say it won't happen again."

"Do you go around punching people very often?"

"Honestly, that's the first sober punch I've tried to throw. He just shouldn't have been that rude to you. It infuriated me." He shook his head. "I thought I had myself under control, that without the alcohol, I could manage my rage. When I drank—if I drink—given the right mood, I'm not beyond picking the fights."

"But you don't drink, right? You're not drinking?"

Her question had neither condemnation nor revulsion in it, and he marveled at her ability to simply be concerned for him. "I'm not drinking. I haven't had a drink in over a year." He'd been tempted recently, and he was sure Charisse had mentioned it to her.

"I know it can make normal people do crazy things. My father was an angry drunk."

She'd never shared that with him. No wonder she feared him. And the truth of it was enough to keep him sober for a lifetime. "Nate never needed a drink to make him mean, and I get my temper from him." What was he doing? Reinforcing her fear? Yes. If it would keep her safe from the type of man he was—the kind who would level a punch even when he was stone-cold sober.

"Then give it back."

Libby's words shook him from his reverie. "Give what back?"

"Nate's temper. You don't have to take what he gives you."

Evan laughed at the child-like simplicity, but the hurt flashing in Libby's beautiful green eyes told him she was dead serious. "How can I do that?"

"Lay it at Jesus' feet and walk away from it. Nate's anger is his problem. You don't need to carry his baggage."

"Easier said than done."

"Anything worth doing is easier said than done. Don't you know that? Besides, I don't think the bag of anger you carry is all that large of one."

"If Gideon hadn't stopped the first punch, I'd have been all over that man. Gideon knew. The first punch fuels the flame of anger, and I explode."

"What did you do to Nate the night he hurt me?"

Evan didn't want to go there. He remained silent. They were following Gideon, and when his friend turned off the exit, Evan tailed him until they pulled up in front of Libby's apartment building.

"What did you do to Nate that night?" Libby asked again.

Evan ran his hand through his hair. "I pushed him off of you. He fell backward against the bed then he went for me. I tried to scoop you up. I thought he'd killed you." He blew air out between puffed cheeks. "I nearly dropped you, but I managed to lay you on the bed. Nate's fist came toward me, and I blocked his punch. He got off balance and the orderly caught him. With the orderly in my way, I couldn't get back to Nate, but make no mistake about it, Libby, I wanted to kill him."

"But you didn't." She reached across and patted his arm before taking her keys from his hand. "You set the baggage down." She opened her car door and stepped outside.

"Libby?" He hurried out of his seat.

She turned and walked backward toward the stairs that would take her to her apartment. "Thank you for the ride."

"Tell me something?"

She stopped moving away from him. "What?"

"How hard was it for you to let that guy get away with what he said?"

"I didn't actually let him get away with it. I said something awful to him."

"Any other girl would have slapped the crap out of him."

Libby shook her head. "He only told the truth, Evan, and he didn't know that those two fools"—she waved at Gideon and Charisse in the car to the right of them—"They set it all up."

He moved to her. She stepped back, and he held up his hands in surrender. If she didn't want his touch, he wouldn't force it upon her. Still, he longed to take her into his arms, to hold her, and to tell her how much he cared. "You can't believe what that jerk said. Libby you're the most—"

She started off.

Exasperation filled him. He was tired of tiptoeing around the truth. He wanted her to know how much he loved her. He wanted her to stop fleeing from him at the slightest misunderstanding. He wanted so much to be the man she needed, and he failed her at every turn.

"You know," he called after her, "you're carrying some baggage that doesn't belong to you either. Somewhere, for whatever reason, someone made you think you're not good enough. Libby—"

She ran up the stairs and into her apartment. The door

closed with a slam.

"You're good enough." He lowered his head and heaved a deep sigh and then moved toward Gideon's car.

"Well?" Gideon met him.

"This is your fault." Evan shook his head, in no mood to talk.

"Me?"

"You set me up, friend, and you set up that creep. Backfired on you, didn't it? I might laugh if Libby hadn't ended up getting hurt again by the moron, by both of you, and by me." He ran a hand through his hair. "Gideon, leave it alone. Libby is frightened of me and of what I could do to her." He started toward the other side of the car but moved back toward his friend. "I mean it."

Gideon nodded. "Sorry."

"No, you're not. You're planning your next step, but I'll be one step ahead of you."

Gideon smiled. "The challenge is on, and you won't see it coming."

Evan stopped with his hand on the door handle. "Thank you for protecting me from my own anger, and let's promise here and now that whatever our next moves are, they won't hurt the woman I love." Who was he kidding? He had to come to an understanding with himself. He had to be the man Libby needed him to be.

He had to lay down his baggage at Jesus' feet and move forward.

But how was he supposed to do something that had been trained into him since he was a small child? He looked up into the face of his smiling friend.

"So you admit it? You're in love with our Libby," Gideon pried.

"God help her, yes, I am, and you need to agree. We're not going to hurt her anymore."

Gideon nodded. "Deal, Evan. The woman I love won't be very happy if I allow something like this to happen again."

Chapter Twelve

Libby dialed the number and closed the phone book, hating the fact she owed yet another apology. Sitting alone in her dark apartment for nearly an hour, she found no peace. Evan had opened up to her, and in her own selfishness, she'd struck back with superficial remarks about the baggage he carried. What did she know of his burden?

With each ring her heart leapt into her throat. Maybe he hadn't returned straight home. Perhaps he'd gone to visit Hope. Her fingers relaxed as she decided to hang up, but the phone clicked. "Hello."

Her grasp on the phone tightened once again. "Evan?"

"Libby, are you okay?"

"Yes. Evan, I'm sorry for treating you so badly this evening. You went out of your way to make sure I arrived home safely. Scott's behavior took me by surprise though I caused it."

"Libby, you didn't cause anything."

"You didn't see what happened." A picture of Scott with the water and the food covering him sprang into her memory. The humor she experienced at Scott's expense was foreign to her thinking, but she couldn't help it. In her attempt to stifle a full-fledged ungodly laugh, a funny little noise escaped.

"Honey, don't cry."

Libby giggled and covered her mouth. *Honey.* She'd hold to that endearment until the day she died.

"Are you laughing?" He laughed with her.

"Oh, Evan. The food and the water, they just seemed determined to land all over him."

"Good. He was a real jerk. Anyone who couldn't see the beauty—"

The loud knock on the other end of the line startled Libby. "You must have company."

"No. Hold on. There's someone outside. Don't go anywhere."

Libby remained silent.

"Libby, don't hang up."

"I'm here. I won't." Her heart soared. Is this why God wouldn't let her rest until she made the call? Did she dare dream that Evan wanted to talk to her. She listened to the faint noises coming over the line. Evan called out to someone for an answer. Libby heard no response. Evan called out again, distress in his voice. Sitting up, she waited to make sure he would be all right.

"Hope, honey, what happened?"

His words shot a dart to her heart. She started to hang up but remembered her promise to stay on the line.

The voices became mumbled. "Hold on, Hope," he said. "Libby," he spoke to her. "I'm sorry. I have to go."

"Sure." She prayed he wouldn't hear the emotion in her voice. "Good night, Evan."

"Libby, can we talk tomorrow? I'm sorry, but I really

have to go to her."

Libby nodded, very aware he could not see. "Good night."

Libby put the phone down, clicked off the only light in the apartment, and sat back in the same seat where she'd sat the last hour. "Oh, God, I'm such a fool for him."

Dropping his phone, Evan ran to the bathroom for a large towel. Hope had done it this time. Anger and fear welled inside him, fighting for position.

"Hope, no." He ran back into the living room. She had fallen back, her eyes closed in drunkenness. Blood from a gash on the back of her skull seeped into the fabric of his couch. He yanked her up by the arm. "Wake up. Hope. Wake up."

She mumbled something about being tired.

Evan pulled her to her feet, and with surprising strength, she swung at him, her diamond ring connecting with his face below his left eye. He pushed back the curse that sprang from his heart. "You do that again, I'll leave you on the floor." An empty threat. First of all, he cared too much for his friend to allow her to die, and secondly, he didn't want a homicide investigation in his home. If Hope continued to lose blood at this rate, the possibility existed.

"Evan, don't you love me anymore? First Danny and

then you. Why?" The smell of Barbados rum tickled Evan's senses and reminded him he wasn't so far removed from the temptation. He could still recognize the distinct aroma of his alcoholic beverage of choice.

He held her against him and pressed the towel to her skull. Her weight fell on him. She'd passed out. Looking toward heaven, he said a silent prayer for strength. He laid her down on the couch, retrieved the phone, and dialed 9-1-1. Then he waited with impatience for the operator to take the information. He barked at the woman when she insisted on knowing how the accident happened. "Ma'am, she knocked on my door. She's bleeding heavily, and she's drunk. I can't get anything out of her. Please have them hurry." He slammed the phone down and moved back to Hope.

He slapped her face as gently as possible, afraid too much force would worsen her injury.

"Huh?" She came to and stared at him for a moment before her eyes rolled back in her head.

"Hope, stay with me. Tell me what happened. Were you in a car accident? How did you get here? Where were you hurt?" His slap was a little harder this time. He needed to keep her awake.

"That hurt," she moaned.

"Listen to me. You're injured and bleeding. What happened?"

Her glazed eyes failed to focus on him. They rolled with her head, left then right, up then down. "Fell."

"Where did you fall?"

"Some bar."

"Where Hope? What bar?"

"On International Drive. Some place. A fight …"

Great. International Drive—tourist trap—hundreds of bars—a long way from his home. "How did you get here?"

"Tiffany dropped me off."

Evan took a deep breath and let it out slowly. "Tiffany's driving?"

"Uh-huh." She lifted her head and looked about her. Evan pressed the towel again, feeling the warm blood seep through the heavy cotton.

"Was she drinking with you?"

"Uh-huh. I talked her into it. Delilah tried to keep her from me, but I won."

"Dear God, please protect Tiffany and anyone in her path."

"God, God, God. Who cares about God?"

"Right now, girl, you should be caring. Do you understand me? I'm worried about you. You might not make it out of this one." The blood ran through his fingers and down his arm. Hope faded once again, and Evan choked on his fear. Where were the paramedics?

Chapter Thirteen

"Come on. Come on." Evan paused for the doors to open then sprang into the emergency room. "Hope Astor. They brought her in by ambulance."

The nurse pushed her hair from her face and looked to him with tired eyes before hitting a button. A buzzer sounded, and a door to the left clicked open for him. Evan ran through, looking left and then right. "Hope Astor, head trauma?" he asked a male nurse.

"Over there." The nurse looked Evan up and down. "Sir, are you okay? Are you injured?"

He'd nearly forgotten the blood covering his clothing even though the smell of aged rust assaulted him in his truck, and he'd almost had to pull over to lose the contents of his stomach. "No. No. It's from her injury."

Evan pulled back the curtain. The doctor and two other nurses looked up. "Are you family?" the doctor asked him.

"No. Good friends. I called the ambulance."

"Do you know how she did this?" The doctor straightened, his eyes looking at Evan's clothes as well.

"She told me she fell in a bar and muttered something about a possible fight."

"I'd say she was slammed against something or someone hit her over the head. This injury didn't result from a simple tumble." The doctor motioned to Evan's clothing. "And you're wearing her blood, how?"

Anger swirled from the innermost part of Evan. He fought to tamp it down. "She showed up at my house bleeding. A friend dropped her off. I got her into the house, and I tried to stop the blood flow."

The doctor nodded. "We need to reach her family."

Evan pulled out his mobile phone and scanned his contacts for Hope's house number. He dialed. After ten rings, he hung up. "I don't have any other number, only her home and her cell phone."

The doctor pulled out his stethoscope and placed it against Hope's chest. "Draw blood. I want to see what she has in her system." He gave Hope his full attention before turning to Evan. "Would you know what she's taken?"

Evan shook his head. "No, sir. Like I said, I wasn't with her. She showed up on my doorstep."

The doctor nodded. "Buckle up, son. We're in for a long night."

Evan stumbled backward, reaching for the bed before his legs gave out.

"You okay?" one of the nurses asked him. "She your girlfriend?"

"Friend. We've known each other a long time."

"We need to get her awake. Maybe she'll respond to you."

"Yeah, sure." He moved to the head of the bed. "Hope," he whispered her name. "Hope, I need you to wake up."

Hope murmured something unintelligible, but her

eyes didn't open.

"Hope, wake up," he said a little louder.

Hope's eyes fluttered and closed.

"I need you to wake up right now. Listen to me."

"Evan." She obeyed him, searching the room.

"I'm here." He took her hand. "I need you to listen. You need to stay awake."

"Where am I?"

"You're in the hospital. They need to treat you, and I can't get in touch with your family."

"Won't come. Gone." Her eyes rolled.

"Hope," he said with such force, the nurse backed away. "Wake up now."

"Tired."

"They're trying to save your life."

"No life …" she let out a sob. "No life to live."

Evan squeezed her hand. He'd been where she was on the night he'd wrecked his old truck. He'd wanted to end the unceasing emotional pain that the booze and the drugs no longer numbed. He touched her face with his hand covered in her dried blood. "Listen to me, Hope. You do have a wonderful life. I want you to have a chance to live it. Come on, darling. Open those pretty blues for me."

Her lids fluttered, and the doctor shined a light in her eyes. Hope blinked.

"Keep them open," Evan pleaded.

The doctor waited. When Hope did as Evan asked, the doctor clasped his hand on Evan's shoulder. "Good job, son."

"You did it." Evan leaned down and whispered in Hope's ear. "Dear God, save this woman's life."

"No God," Hope mumbled. "Evan, no God."

"There is a God, Hope, and He loves you. Hang on. Please hang on."

A clamor of activity filled the hallway on the other side of the curtain. "Tiffany. We're here for Tiffany Duvall," a woman cried. "Where's my baby?"

Elsa Duvall.

Evan took a deep breath. He released his hold on Hope's hand and dared to part the curtain. Jacob Duvall, Tiffany's father, came through the same door Evan had entered moments before. Seeing Evan, he stepped toward him. "Were you involved in any of this?" The man clenched his hands into fists. "Evan, so help me …" He stared at the blood on Evan's clothing.

"No, Mr. Duvall. I'm here with Hope. Tiffany dropped her off at my house. Hope was injured somehow in a bar."

"Hope wasn't in the car?"

"No, sir."

"Jacob! No!" Elsa's wail filled the emergency room. "Jacob." The woman staggered out from behind the curtain. She fell into her husband's arms. "She's gone. Our baby's gone."

Evan helped Jacob find a chair and together they made the woman sit.

For a long moment, she seemed to fade from reality. Then she looked up at Evan. "You!" Elsa sprang at him.

Her fists pounded Evan's chest. He braced himself, allowing the woman to spend her grief on him. "All the partying, the drinking, the nights she didn't come home. You're to blame, Evan Carter." Her hand fell across Evan's cheek with the force of someone so anguished she could most likely kill him if given the chance.

Evan didn't dispute her allegations toward him, didn't try to soften the blows. He deserved every one of them. When the woman tired, she fell against him, sobbing. Evan held a trembling Elsa Duvall close to him, allowing her to spend her grief.

"Elsa, honey, he wasn't with them." Jacob pulled his wife into his arms.

Evan stared at the blood that transferred from his clothing on to Elsa's expensive blouse. He may not have been with them, but Tiffany's death and the blood on him and on Elsa were as much his fault as it was Hope's.

Elsa blinked. "How are you here?" She covered her face with her hands. "My baby. My beautiful baby girl." She lifted her head and screamed at the top of her lungs.

"Mom?" Daniel Duvall ran toward them. Evan's old friend looked as if he'd dressed hastily. His hair was unkempt; his shirt wasn't tucked in.

A nurse came from the curtain behind them where apparently lay the dead body of Tiffany Duvall— beautiful, bubbly Tiffany. Evan would forever remember the bounce in her step and the sway of her dark ponytail.

"Dr. Duvall, we're sorry for your family's loss," the nurse said to Daniel.

Daniel's face contorted with grief. "Tiff?" He looked to Evan and then advanced on him. "What have you done?" He gripped Evan by the shirt in the same way Evan had grabbed the man at Gideon's house earlier.

"Daniel, I'm sorry. This shouldn't have happened."

"I thought—the last time we ran into each other you said you were sober. You said you were staying away from Hope. How could you let this happen to my sister?"

Evan shook his head. He wanted to tell Daniel he couldn't have prevented it, that he didn't know Tiffany had dropped Hope off at his house. But the truth was, Evan would forever blame himself for Tiffany's death. How many times in the past had they all been drunk and acted as carelessly as Hope and Tiffany had behaved this evening. He'd never tried to reach out to Daniel's sister. And he'd never made Hope listen to him.

"An accident." Jacob pulled a handkerchief from his pocket and wiped moist eyes. "She hit a tree at a high rate of speed. Daniel, Evan wasn't with them."

Daniel released Evan.

Evan stumbled backward.

"Hope?" Daniel ran his hands through his hair. "Where is Hope?" Daniel straightened, his eyes wide. Color drained from his face.

Evan didn't wonder that Daniel would ask. Hope's family and the Duvall's were neighbors. The girls had grown up together. Tiffany rarely did anything without Hope. And Evan had long suspected that Daniel loved Hope Astor and much as Evan knew Hope loved Daniel.

"Hope was injured in a bar. More than likely, she got

herself into a brawl," Evan managed to say. "She has a large gash on her head. She's losing a lot of blood. I'm not sure she'll make it."

"And you weren't with her?" Daniel's jaw clenched. "Don't lie to me, Evan. My sister is dead. You didn't get them into the middle of one of your fights?"

How many times tonight would he have to explain? "No, Daniel. I was home. Tiffany dropped Hope off at my house. I never saw Tiff. I'm sorry. I didn't hear them drive up. I was on the phone. Hope must have fallen against the door. I found her on my doorstep. Tiffany had already driven off. Believe me, I wouldn't have allowed her to drive away."

Daniel stumbled toward Evan. He clasped a hand on Evan's shoulder. "I'm sorry."

Evan nodded his understanding.

Daniel pushed away. "I want to see my sister."

Elsa sobbed into her hands, and Daniel bent in front of her. "Mom, I'm sorry." He touched his mother's face.

"She told me yesterday—just yesterday—that something wonderful had happened in her life recently, and before that, I'd seen this change. She wasn't out every night. She'd get up early and join some girls for coffee."

Libby. Delilah. Charisse. Evan closed his eyes. Could he dare believe Tiffany was home in heaven?

"I'm really sorry for your loss." Evan nodded and started away.

"I pray to God Hope dies," Elsa Duvall spat the words.

Evan stared at the grief-stricken woman. "You may get your wish, Mrs. Duvall, but I'm praying she doesn't, and I'll continue to pray for your family. If you need anything, please let me know."

"Are you okay?" For the first time, Daniel seemed to take full notice of Evan's condition.

"I'm fine. This is Hope's blood. She lost a lot of it."

"That much, and she's still alive?"

Evan swallowed. Hard. Daniel was a doctor. He should know these things. "As I said, it's a head injury. You know how those go, but the doctor did tell me it would be a long night."

"Are you still seeing her?" Daniel asked.

"Hope and I haven't dated for a long while, Danny." Evan stared at the man.

Daniel's body shook as if he were trying very hard to stay in control. "I hope they'll be able to save her, but I pray to God I never see her face again."

Evan never knew roots of bitterness to grow so quickly. "If the three of you are looking for someone to blame, your mother is right to put the burden on me. You know I used to party like this." His lips trembled. "Who knows, if I'd tried a little harder to get them out of the lifestyle, Tiffany might be alive today." He darted behind the curtain and into Hope's room as the aide came to take the unconscious Hope for an MRI.

He sat hard in a chair. Maybe if he'd taken the time when Hope called him from the beach, if he'd gone to pick them up, he could have talked to both of them about the God he served.

Evan shook his head. He hadn't served God well, not where Hope and Tiffany were concerned.

He leaned forward and cried into his blood-stained hands.

Evan returned to the hospital early the next morning to find Hope sleeping upstairs in a private room. He'd showered and changed from his bloodied clothes, yet he still felt soiled by the ugliness of what occurred to his two friends. In the time spent alone, he tried to reason himself out of the equation, but God continued to remind him he had some blame in this as well.

He'd gotten behind the wheel of a vehicle more than once when he'd consumed alcohol. During his last such drive, despite trying to do himself bodily harm, he'd only wrecked his car. Tiffany's mistake cost her life. As a result of his gaffe, God brought new life and new friendships, Gideon, Charisse—and Libby.

At the thought of Libby, his heart broke. How could someone so sweet and innocent ever love someone who caused so much havoc in the lives of others?

Evan sat in the chair beside the bed of his sleeping friend. He bowed his head. "Lord, I have no right to judge her. I've been a part of her past. I know You love her. She needs You now. Let something I do or say speak Your love to her. Break her heart and make it new like You've done mine. Mend the hearts of Tiffany's loved ones.

Mend my heart, Father. Please mend Hope."

Evan placed his pain at the Lord's feet. He wiped the tears away time after time. "I love you, Lord." The words flowed through his mind and welled up within him, and his heart opened his mouth in praise. "Words are not enough to fathom the depths my love flows for You."

Nor you the love I have for you.

The words seemed to come from outside of him, as if the Father himself had wrapped His arms around Evan.

Nate.

At a time like this, why had Nate even come to mind? Nate was nowhere in this equation, and besides, the distance between Nate and the love of God spanned as far as the east from the west.

No sooner had the thought entered his mind did he remember the words of the Psalmist. *As far as the east is from the west, so far hath he removed our transgressions from us.*

"Nate's transgressions have not been removed from me. Lord, I still have the scars."

And I bear yours.

Evan opened his eyes. He stared at the bed for a long moment drinking in the truth of what the Lord was calling him to do. "Lord," he cried. "Strengthen me for the love I have to share with Nate."

"Evan?"

He pushed himself to sit up straight. "Morning, Hope."

Hope blinked. "Are you okay? Did I do that to you?" She pointed to a spot just below her own eye. He touched the sore area on his face where she'd clocked him the night before. It went well with his hurting cheek were Elsa had slapped him.

"Yeah, but don't worry about it."

"You were praying?"

"I was praying."

"For me?" she asked, her eyes wide.

He nodded, "And for me. How's your head?"

"Do you think God heard you?"

"I know He heard." Evan ran his hand along the sheet on her bed.

"How can you know?"

"He's given you another chance."

"What do you mean?" She tried to push herself further up on the bed.

"Do you remember anything about last night?" He slipped his hand under her arm and helped her to gain a hold. Then he repositioned her pillow behind her.

Hope laid her head back. "I feel sick."

"You were injured in a bar. You had Tiffany drop you off. Want to tell me what happened?"

She looked above his head, winced, and then rubbed her eyes. When she pulled away, she stared at the IV there. "I don't remember."

He'd had many nights like that, so he understood. "I prayed for you last night. God saved your life."

Hope continued to stare at the IV, and then she looked around her at the other wires attached to her. "I think the doctors saved my life."

Evan bent forward, his face close to hers. "Don't get arrogant with me. God protected you on your little drive to my place. Tiffany wrecked her car after she dumped you off on my doorstep."

"She was fine." Hope flitted her hand in the air as if to abate his concern, but her gaze never settled on him.

"Look at me, Hope."

She turned her head, wincing as she did so.

"After she left you, she wrapped her car around a tree."

She blinked. "Is she hurt? Is she here?"

"She's dead."

Hope gasped. "She's not. Evan, you're lying, trying to frighten me."

Evan softened his voice. "She died downstairs. While God spared your life in one room, Tiffany lost hers in another. Elsa, Jacob, Daniel: they were all here."

An unreadable expression crossed Hope's face. She closed her eyes and leaned her head back. Tears trickled down her face in soundless grief. After several minutes, she wiped the back of her IV-less hand across her eyes. "Evan, where are my parents?"

He sat back in the chair. "I can't find them."

Silence stretched between them, long and uncomfortable. Evan prayed for the right words to say and the right moment to say them.

"You think if I'd died last night, I'd be in hell, don't you? Well, you're wrong. I think when we die, we're buried and that's it. There's nothing else."

"I used to think that, too. That's why I lived so hard. I

wanted to get rid of the pain, and if I had to continue to live, I made the choice to fuel myself with the alcohol and the reaction I had to it."

"So what? We need to get rid of the pain somehow. We're not like your little friend Libby who has no troubles or concerns. She just goes around everywhere spreading sunshine, doesn't she?"

Libby sure had gotten under Hope's skin. Good. "You don't know anything about Libby Overstreet. By God's grace and mercy, she didn't take the same path we did, but she is filled with pain. I didn't realize how much until recently."

"She lives in a different world."

"She lives in the same world you and I do. She's just risen above it. Libby and I share the same faith. And Hope, I love her. She's off limits to any schemes you might have. I care for you, but I'm praying God will make me into the man Libby deserves. I have to have faith." From where had that come? He'd just gone against his very belief that his love for Libby would only hurt her, and he'd spoken his thoughts aloud—to Hope.

Death and near death. That's what made him say it.

"Faith? What is that? It's a belief in fairy tales. I told Delilah …" Her words trailed off, and she lifted her hand to her head, closing her eyes tightly.

Libby said something to him about fairy tales, how hers weren't the happily-ever-after kind. If he had his way, her life would be an endless happily-ever-after. If he could just untangle himself from his past so that he could catch up with her when she ran from him.

"Did you hear me, Evan? What is faith?"

He focused on her question. How could he put it so simply that a woman with a concussion could understand? "Faith is believing that God's Word is not a myth but truth, and one of God's many truths is that we all die a physical death. If you belong to Jesus, the bad part is over. When your journey on earth is done, you'll dwell with Him in heaven. If you don't take this second chance God's given you to know Him personally, and you die, you're going to face something far worse than what you faced last night."

"I just told you I don't think there's a hell."

"So, we're at a standstill. I know if you continue on without faith, you'll go to hell, and you don't believe in hell. If there's the slightest chance Jesus holds the key separating fact from fiction—and Hope, He does— why would you take a chance on your being right? Tiffany doesn't have another chance. You do."

That was tough. Even he had to admit.

The clattering of breakfast trays gave him an excuse to step away, but he never took his eyes from her.

Hope's gaze followed him while the woman set the liquid diet in front of her.

"Yummy." He smirked at the unappetizing lumps of Jell-O, the yellow soup-like substance, and the cup of hot water and tea bag.

She pushed the tray away and then raised her hand to the bandage.

He pushed the tray back toward her. "You need to eat."

"Why are you here? Why do you care about my belief in God? What's it to you?"

"I'm here because we both lost a friend to a senseless death. And no matter how hard I try to fight it, Hope, I care about you. We've been friends a long time, and I can't stand to see you so miserable. I don't know why you think your life is all that bad. Before I became a Christian, from where I stood, you had it good—a loving mother and father, good friends in Tiffany and Delilah. And what about Daniel? You lived a charmed life, and I was lucky to be along for the ride. When I accepted Christ, I saw the emptiness in the lives we led. I know why I turned to the drugs and alcohol, but I never understood why you did."

"There wasn't anything better to do, Evan. Life is boring. What more is there? Life is an endless circle of nothing. And Danny, he's moved on."

Evan was probably the cause of Daniel's absence in Hope's life. "It can be an endless circle of joy if you put your trust in the right One. No matter what comes. No matter who moves on without us, we can have happiness."

"I don't understand how you can have any pleasure, not the way you were raised. I know the horrors you faced, Evan." She fumbled with the wrapping containing the silverware and napkin and then giving up, she slammed it down by her tray.

He sat on the bed and picked up the wrapped utensils,

opening them with one tear. "It's nothing I've done and everything that Christ has done for me." He pulled out the contents and handed them to her. "Do you ever feel at peace?"

She bit her lip and gave a cautious shake of her head.

"I do now," he declared. "Yeah, sometimes I take my attention off the Lord, or I want something I shouldn't have, and my peace shatters, but all I have to do is put my eyes back on Jesus. He calms my world."

With a shaky hand, she dipped the spoon into the soup but allowed it to fall back into the bowl. Tears pooled in her eyes. "If what you say is true, Tiffany could be in hell."

Evan picked up the bowl and spoon. She allowed him to feed her several spoonsful before she turned her head away from him.

"Would you like me to leave so you can rest?" He placed the bowl on the tray.

"Please don't leave. I'm all alone. Tiffany …"

"Tiffany." He agreed with her grief simply by repeating their friend's name. He sat in the chair once again.

Hope turned her head to the window and closed her eyes. Tears slid down and moistened her pillow. "Thank you for staying."

"You're welcome. Sleep and I'll be here when you wake."

"I'll think about what you told me."

"That's a big step. Do you want me to try to call your family again?"

"No," she whispered. "Despite the picture you want to paint of my family, they don't care."

When Hope's breathing fell into rhythm, Evan took her food tray away and pulled the covers over her. Then he leaned back and closed his eyes. The memory of Libby's sweet mirth from the night before brought a smile to his face.

What would it be like to hear her laughter every day? He opened his eyes. His thoughts had turned from Jesus and toward a desire outside his reach. He leaned forward, his hands clasped in front of him, and he stared at the floor. The *tap-tap* of shoes on the hospital flooring alerted him that someone approached. The four-inch spiked heels could only belong to one person. Still, he needed to pray. "Lord, I know it's an unreasonable request, but I love Libby."

Delilah clasped a hand upon his shoulder, startling him. "Libby's not an unreasonable request. You're a good man, and by God's goodness, she can make you even better."

He looked up. "Delilah, I'm sorry I didn't think to let you know."

She waved off his apology. "Danny called. He said you were here, and you probably needed someone. I'd have been here sooner, but I had arraignments and needed to get Gid to fill in for me. He had to finish up a sentencing before he could help. They're going to go over and let Libby know about Tiffany later this afternoon."

Eyes red and puffy, Delilah had never seemed so

vulnerable before. Evan jumped to his feet and made her sit in his chair. "Dee, I'm sorry."

"I know what you're thinking, Ev. We all had something to do with Tiffany's death."

He nodded.

"While a tragic loss, it's not as bad as you think." Delilah dug into her purse and pulled out a handkerchief.

"I never took the chance to tell her about the Lord."

Delilah blew her nose. "And everything revolves around what Evan does and doesn't do. Well, let me tell you something, Mr. Carter. Tiffany and I had some long talks about her soul, and she accepted Christ the day she died. Don't ask me why she went out drinking last night. I have my suspicions." She rolled her eyes toward the sleeping woman in the bed. "Tiffany never was one to stand up against our strong-willed friend. And if you mention the proverbial pot and kettle, I'm going to take my spiked heels off and give you a matching mark under your other eye."

Evan smiled and shook his head. "We can't blame, Hope."

"And we can't blame ourselves, but God has placed someone into both our messed up lives, and Tiffany is in heaven tonight because that special someone led me to Christ, and the Lord used me to share His love with Tiffany. You're a fool if you let one more day pass without telling Libby exactly how you feel. What am I saying, Evan? You're an idiot for making my friend so miserable."

Evan shook his head. "I'm not bringing her into this

mess. Not right now. I'll continue to pray that the Lord will open a door, but right now, He's closed it, because we need to see Hope through."

"I'll pray for you, too. Libby is a dear, but sometimes her little world doesn't open her heart up to the possibility that someone might care about her."

"Don't talk about her like that."

"She doesn't see life the way we see it, Ev. You have to know that."

"She sees the goodness in everyone." He smiled.

Delilah touched his hand. "That's it. She does see it in everyone. Everyone but herself."

Libby hadn't slept the night before. Like a fool she'd believed Evan would return last night's call. She'd gone to work, and the day dragged. Now home, all she wanted to do was fall into bed and forget everything: Evan, her loneliness, the despair.

She walked inside, dropping her keys on her kitchen counter. Should she eat, take a shower, or simply climb into bed? "A shower." She mustered some energy. "Then I'll read until I fall asleep."

A knock at the door startled her.

"Libby, it's us," Gideon called. "We need to talk to you."

She pulled open the door. "What is it?"

Charisse's eyes were swollen and red. "There's been

an accident, and Delilah wanted you to hear it from us."

"Evan," she breathed his name. Why else would they be her if not for …? "Not Evan." She backed away from them, her hands covering her face. What would she do if they told her he was gone? No. She shook her head. She wouldn't believe it. Her throat tightened. She couldn't breathe. Her heart ached with each slow beat. She stumbled backward, reaching for the wall. "Please … say he's okay."

Charisse hurried to her side. "Evan's safe."

Charisse's words took a moment to soak in. Libby's heartbeat returned to normal, and she breathed evenly. "Don't you ever do that to me again."

Gideon led both women into the living room and made them sit. "I'm going to order pizza while Charisse gives you the news."

Charisse motioned for Gideon to lean down. When he did, she kissed his cheek. "Give us a minute. And no anchovies. I don't have the strength to pick them off." She lifted a sad smile to him. When he moved away, she grasped Libby's hand. "Maybe now isn't time for pizza, but he's better at these things when he can keep busy."

"What is it?" Libby asked.

"Tiffany had an accident last night."

Libby jumped to her feet. "Is she in the hospital? We don't need to order pizza. We need to go—"

Charisse shook her head.

Libby sank to the couch. "She's dead?"

Charisse nodded.

"Where's Delilah?"

"She and Evan are with someone who needs her right now. They'd be here if they could."

"That's right. Tiffany was Evan's friend, too." Libby looked at her hands. "Have you talked to him? Is he okay?"

"He's hurting, of course, but Delilah says he's doing fine. She said to tell you she's watching out for him."

Libby didn't protest, nor did she want to lie to Charisse. Truth was, the sudden fear of losing Evan to death had etched him deeper into her heart. "Delilah will take care of him."

Gideon hung up the phone and sat on Libby's coffee table. He reached for each of their hands. "Let's pray."

Libby bowed her head. Where was Hope? No one had mentioned her. She'd been with Evan the night before, and Hope and Tiffany were very close. This had to have affected her deeply. Delilah was close to Hope. Hope was very close to Evan. She opened her eyes as Gideon prayed.

Delilah and Evan were with Hope.

Did Gideon and Charisse think her so unreasonable she wouldn't understand?

Or did they know Evan had always loved Hope?

Libby took a quivering breath. How selfish could she be? This wasn't like her. *Dear God, draw Hope close to You. Help Evan and Delilah minister to her. Give Evan the desires of his heart, please, Father. Help him to love Hope, and bring Hope to You.*

"In Jesus' name, Amen." Gideon's prayer and Libby's silent prayer ended at the same time.

Libby touched Charisse's face, moist with tears. "I can't imagine how Hope, Delilah, and Evan must feel right now. If I lost my best friend, I wouldn't be able to function."

"Yes, you would." Charisse smiled through her tears. "Because you'd have to take care of my big fella and the little guy I'd leave behind."

"I've said some things to you both over the last couple of months that would forever weigh on my heart if I didn't take this chance to tell you how sorry I am and how much I love you."

Gideon leaned forward, his arms opened wide. "We're family. That's how it goes." He wrapped Charisse and Libby in his embrace.

Family.

Libby wasn't so alone after all.

Chapter Fourteen

Libby sat in the funeral home pew beside Charisse and stared at the closed casket and the mourners taking the time to console the Duvall family. She ran her hand along the coarse fabric of the seat. "A parent shouldn't have to bury a child." Those murmured words seemed to encircle the room along with the declaration, "She had so much life yet to live."

Libby dug in her purse for a Kleenex and wiped her eyes.

Gideon sat, one arm draped over the side of the pew, his other on Charisse's shoulders. He tapped Libby on her shoulder and nodded as Evan walked past them.

Evan joined others in line to speak to Tiffany's family.

Libby straightened her black skirt. Evan looked very handsome in his gray suit, but his shoulders were drooped, and he rubbed a hand over his eyes before turning and scanning the crowd. His gaze settled on her, and he offered her a sad smile, pointing to the spot beside her and back to him. She nodded and sat straighter.

"How you doing?" Gideon leaned around Charisse to speak to Libby.

"I'm fine." She ran the Kleenex under her eyes and smiled up at Delilah who moved to stand beside Gideon, arms crossed over her chest, the toe of her left shoe tapping the carpet.

"What?" Gideon raised a brow.

"Move over." She bumped him with her knee.

Charisse turned to Libby. They both shared a smile. Who would win this new war—fought during a funeral no less?

"Dee, you can sit on the other end," Gideon said, turning so Delilah could move by.

"I want to sit here."

"Children." Libby stood and moved down a seat. "Delilah, sit here."

Delilah didn't move.

"Oh, for goodness' sakes, Gideon." Charisse moved down. "We're at a funeral."

Gideon looked up at Delilah and winked. Delilah smiled and moved in between Charisse and Libby, making Charisse scoot back toward her husband. "Hey." She reached for Libby's hand and gave it a tight squeeze.

"Delilah, I'm so sorry," Libby said, "but I'm rejoicing because we know where Tiffany is today."

"Where's Hope?" Charisse turned to look behind them.

Delilah shook her head. "Elsa Duvall asked her not to attend."

Evan made his way back down the aisle. He shook Gideon's hand and then kissed Charisse and Delilah's cheeks as he scooted past them. When he came to Libby, he hesitated for a moment. Libby looked away to alleviate his embarrassment. He was probably horrified at the thought of his lips on her, even to comfort her as a friend.

He sat beside her.

"I'm sorry, Evan, and I'm sorry Hope isn't able to be here," Libby said.

"She's not well, so she probably couldn't come anyway." He straightened his suit jacket.

"Is there anything I can do?"

He offered her another sad smile. "No, but thank you."

Libby stared straight ahead.

Delilah's hand in Libby's trembled, and Libby slipped her arm around her. Delilah leaned against Libby. "If not for you."

"If not for God." Libby held to Delilah, and the brash judge sobbed against her.

"I love you, Libby," Delilah whispered, "for your humility, and your innocence, and for your strength."

Evan stared straight ahead, clenching his jaw to hide his emotion.

I love you, too, Libby. For your humility, your innocence, and your strength.

And he missed her. Since Hope's accident, he and Delilah traded shifts caring for their injured friend. Evan had hired an aide to care for Hope at Delilah's place so they could attend the funeral. The nurse practitioner had also agreed to help him and Delilah with Hope's care until

Hope got on her feet.

Evan had finally reached Hope's mother. He looked around the room. The Astors had apparently decided to not attend the funeral, either by choice or because Elsa didn't want them here. When he'd called the home and finally received an answer, Connie Astor held to her cold and self-righteous demeanor. She said she'd told Hope she needed to settle down. Maybe *this* would bring Hope to her senses and give her the reason she needed to settle down. Evan had reminded Connie that *this* was the death of Hope's best friend, the daughter or a couple who'd lived across the street from the Astors for years. Nothing he said, defrosted the coolness in Connie's tone.

Evan now understood what Hope meant when she said her parents didn't care.

He reached behind Libby and patted Delilah's back. They'd become close over the last few days as they passed in and out of her apartment. He stayed with Hope during the mornings since his crew could work with very little supervision. When Delilah came home in the early afternoon, he'd leave and check the progress of the various jobs he had going both in and out of the office, and then he'd fall to sleep with visions of Libby dancing in his dreams, only to wake the next day to start the progress over again.

He needed a break, just some time to not think about Hope's injuries, her family's abandonment, and Tiffany's death.

He planned to talk his fellow mourners into lunch following the funeral. He and Delilah could use the break, and he was sure they weren't all that welcome at the Duvall home. Besides, he had a surprise for Libby, one he couldn't wait to share. It had been less than a week, but to him it seemed a lifetime had passed since he looked into Libby's beautiful green eyes.

They were moist with tears then as well. Tears he had caused. At least today, her sadness wasn't caused by his wrongdoing.

Or was it?

He winced.

Delilah had reminded him constantly of God's forgiveness, but his past had collided with this present, and he did hold some blame. He'd lost a dear friend, and Libby lost a new one.

He sat forward, elbows on his knees, face in his hands, and stared at the floor.

Libby rested her hand on his arm, and he turned to look up at her. "I'm so sorry," he whispered. "I didn't mean to put you through this, to have things end like this." He placed his hand over hers.

Libby's lips quivered. "Evan, it's okay. I know you love her."

Evan nodded and lowered his head. He did love Tiffany, her vibrancy, her ability to make people feel welcome and loved. She was a peacemaker. How many times had she been able to calm the fury inside of them— often a fury Hope had instigated toward another?

When he closed his eyes, his tears fell to the ground at his feet.

Libby's world tilted off its axis. She'd made the decision to stop this give and take in her heart. She'd wanted to provide Evan with release. Hope needed him so desperately.

But now that she'd said the words she couldn't take back, Libby felt as if she were drowning in hopelessness.

She pressed her hand to her chest and told herself to drink in the air, but her heart had stopped—but no, it couldn't have. It pounded so hard against her chest. She ached from it.

Why, if she uttered the words to make things easier on Evan, did she not brace her heart for his expected response?

Breathe.

She'd opened the door, and the worst had happened.

Breathe.

Evan admitted he loved Hope.

Breathe.

She'd dreamed it all up, taking his friendly attention and turning it into the possibility of a full-blown love affair.

Breathe.

He would never be hers. Never.

Stop breathing. Stop breathing.

The pastor moved to the podium.

Delilah cried against Libby again, and Libby concentrated on helping her friend. She listened to the eulogy, and when he called for people who'd like to say something about Tiffany, Evan stood.

She couldn't hear him over the swooshing in her ears. Delilah squeezed her hand, and when Evan sat, he placed his hand over hers once again. Did they both realize she was sinking in self-pity? What a terrible way to behave at a funeral.

As the pastor gave an invitation, several people stood. Libby would normally rejoice, but she'd moved from pain into numbness.

The funeral ended, and one by one the rows cleared. Libby walked behind Delilah to the front lobby and sidestepped her and made it through the exit.

"Libby," Evan called to her. "I thought we could have lunch, the five of us."

She forced herself to look at him, shielding her eyes with her hand to keep the sun's glare at bay. "No. Please go ahead. I have to go."

Not a lie. If she didn't go, they'd all know the depth of her despair. She couldn't face them—any of them—for one more second.

"Are you sure?" he asked.

She nodded and walked way, fighting hard to keep from breaking into a run.

Evan walked back into the funeral home. What had he done this time to make her scurry away so quickly?

Charisse slipped her arm in his. "You know, it hasn't been that long since her mother's death, and Libby didn't take time to grieve. Maybe Tiffany's funeral opened the door for her to release some of the feelings about her mom."

"No," he told her. "There's something more."

"Gideon and I will drive by and see she's okay."

"No, dear wife," Gideon said. "We've been hovering over her too much. We need to let Libby think things out." He pointed to Evan. "And you stay away from her, too."

"We should tell her about Hope," Evan said. "She asked me about her, and I told her she wasn't well. I hated lying to her."

"She isn't well. You didn't lie, and would you like to add to Libby's burden by her insistence on helping with Hope's care? Hope would tear her to shreds right now." Delilah wrapped him in a hug. "Thanks for sharing the story of how Libby's love and concern for others seeped into Tiffany's life so we know where Tiffany is today. Powerful testimony."

"I don't think she heard a word I said." Evan shook his head. "How can I help her if she runs from me every time I try to talk to her?"

Gideon hugged Charisse to him. "You need to keep talking, buddy, until it breaks through."

"If you all have a few minutes, I'd like to show you something. Then maybe we can grab some lunch. Delilah and I need a break."

Gideon looked at his watch. "I have two hours before

I need to get back for a hearing. You, Dee?"

"I cleared my afternoon calendar."

"Charisse, do you have all your homework done?" Gideon teased.

"Yes, I do."

"We're all yours, Evan." Gideon nodded. "What are we going to see?"

Evan smiled. "The first of what I hope will be many happy-ever-afters for Libby Overstreet."

If he could only get her to stop running from him.

Libby had thought about going home and curling up to die, but instead, she ended up at the nursing home, sitting beside Scarlet Trevetti in the dining room. Libby picked at the food on her tray.

Scarlet placed a trembling hand over Libby's. "Libby, girl, what's wrong? And don't tell me nothing. There's pain written all over your face."

Libby tried to push a smile in place, but she couldn't do it. "Nothing for you to worry over, Scarlet."

"How's Nate Carter's boy these days? I haven't seen him around here very much. I thought you might be keeping him company."

"You know everyone in this place, don't you?"

Scarlet put a finger to her lips. "I've known Nate Carter longer than most. He's a mean cuss. I heard what happened to you. He should have been locked up long ago."

"He isn't responsible …"

"What he did to that handsome son of his—the only one of the bunch he raised that ever did anything good. Have you seen his scars?"

Libby shook her head. "I don't want to talk about Evan, Scarlet."

"Well, he don't know me from nobody." She picked up her milk and took a sip through the straw. Setting the small carton down, she looked away as if remembering. "His momma was a glutton for punishment, and she condemned her boys to the same. Denise would blame his temper on everyone and everything but where it belonged. She should have gotten those kids away from him, but she kept hanging on."

"Scarlet, I don't know how you know about Evan's family, but we shouldn't be talking about this." Yes, Libby longed to know what Evan truly suffered, but she only wanted to hear it if Evan wanted to share it with her.

"Fine." Scarlet pushed some corn onto a fork with her biscuit. She ate it and rolled her eyes. "This here is some good eating."

Libby managed to smile, and Scarlet winked at her.

"But I am curious," Libby said. "How do you know the Carters so well? Why wouldn't Evan know you?"

"You won't be telling none of my secrets now, will you?" Scarlet put down her fork. When Libby didn't answer, Scarlet nudged her with her elbow. "I'm only fooling you. This tough old bird retired as a deputy sheriff in another life. I got called out to the Carter house many a time by fearful neighbors when the Carter boys were young'uns. Classic signs of abuse and denial … all of 'em, including the sons. That one you've set your sights on, Libby girl, he was the only one of them that didn't see the inside of a jail."

Libby bit her lip. By Evan's own admission, he had been arrested once for DUI, but Scarlet didn't need to know that.

Libby blinked. What had the woman said? "Scarlet, how did you know?"

"That you're in love with the boy?" She cackled. "You have a friend who's shared some things with me. He visits Nate sometimes, and they let him in to see him. The Jamaican nurse, she introduced him to me. But, Libby girl, the way you look at each other, it's enough to make me believe that there is a God, and He's pulling the strings to tie the two of you together."

Libby straightened. Just who was this friend sharing things about her and Evan? She closed her eyes. She'd have two likely suspects and a clue that the person was a male, and a pretty good-sized one if they let him in to visit with Nate.

Not too hard to figure out. Gideon was such a—such a romantic at heart. She had half a mind to tell Evan about Gideon's interference—if she could ever face Evan again.

Still, Libby had been so focused on her own pain that she'd forgotten that here was an elderly woman who'd never met the Lord. "Scarlet, we've talked about God before. He is very real."

"Yeah, yeah, yeah. Let me tell you something. If there is a God, I'll listen to what He has to say, if He'll let me talk to that boy. I'd like to tell Evan Carter a thing or two I've learned in life. I don't mean ever to embarrass him. I'd never tell him how I know about him or his family, but that boy is good. One thing I do know. You ought to hold fast to that one, and never let him go."

Libby bit her lips so hard she thought they'd bleed. She wasn't going to tell Scarlet that Evan loved Hope, and Libby had nothing to hold to. She patted Scarlet's hand. "I'll pray you get the opportunity to talk to Evan then, especially if you'll keep your promise to God.

Chapter Fifteen

Libby stared out the florist shop window. Intermittent rain kept downtown traffic sparse for a Saturday morning, and few customers entered the store. Still, working seemed much better than a lonely morning at home. She planned to spend her afternoon at the nursing home visiting with some of her friends there. She had no special gifts for them today and hoped her smile would be enough.

A week had passed since Tiffany's funeral, and Libby's behavior in front of her friends still haunted her. She needed to grow up, to move on, and forget about Evan Carter—or at least learn to stay in the same room with him without running away from the fact he'd chosen another over her.

What was she thinking? He hadn't *chosen* someone different. Libby had only dreamed he could love her. From the very day they'd been introduced, she could have guessed Hope was the woman Evan loved.

The door opened and the shop's owner entered to handle the afternoon shift. Small drops of rain dotted Margie's salt and pepper hair, clinging to the excessive amount of hairspray the older woman used to maintain her hairstyle.

"I filled two call-in orders. They're being delivered

now. The shelves are restocked, and I rearranged the back room like you asked." Libby began to reorganize the items on the counter, moving pens and paper out of her boss's way.

Margie moved the receipt book and tidied the same papers Libby set aside.

"Is something wrong?" Libby cringed, awaiting an answer that would match the taut lines on Margie's face.

Margie lifted the glasses she wore on a chain around her neck and placed them on her pointed nose. "Libby, when I hired you, I indicated I had high hopes for an increase in business."

"Yes." Libby stepped closer.

"Don't look like I'm going to shoot you in the foot or something." Margie offered her first smile. "The hours might not be here for you, sweetheart. That's all I'm saying. If something comes across, and you need to leave, I wanted to let you know I won't hold it against you. I'd hate losing you. You're a very good worker."

Libby nodded. "Don't worry. I have some money set aside. I'd planned to invest in a business, but it didn't work out. You just tell me when you want me to come in."

"We'll try to keep your weekly hours." Margie's shoulders relaxed. "I might not have you come in on Saturdays."

Great. Now she'd face an entire day of loneliness each week. "I appreciate your honesty." Libby nodded, trying to place a look of confidence on her face. "You've been very kind to me, and I'm gaining valuable knowledge." She picked up her purse and waved her good-bye.

Outside, a soft, misty rain clung to her skin, and she inhaled. Even the exhaust fumes from the downtown thoroughfare failed to mask the aroma of warm air against an afternoon shower.

If all Libby had to offer to the nursing home residents was her smile, she needed time to replace the disappointment she suspected had seeped into the lines of her face. She started down the street toward Java Lava. She only needed something small to tide her over until she rounded up some leftovers at home.

Ahead of her, Evan opened the door of the coffee shop for Hope and ushered her inside. Libby stopped.

She steeled her emotions and moved forward, one foot in front of the other until she made it inside. A test of her new resolution to face challenges like a grownup.

Evan stood in line. Hope had taken a seat.

Libby took her place in line behind him.

"A strawberry smoothie, a large black coffee, and two of those banana muffins," Evan ordered.

She waited, looking everywhere but at the back of Evan's head.

Evan turned. "Libby."

Cringing inside, she forced herself to look at him.

He leaned against the counter. "Give the lady your order. I'm buying."

"No, that's okay." She cast an uneasy glance in Hope's direction.

"I won't hear of it. Sit with Hope and me."

"Ma'am?" the woman at the counter asked.

"Add this to my total," Evan said.

Libby fought the sigh she wanted to give. "A sweet tea and a zucchini muffin."

Evan waited until all the food was placed on a tray, and then he coaxed her to the table with him.

Hope wore a baseball cap. Strange as that seemed, something else was different. Evan pulled out the chair for Libby and doled out the food and drinks from the tray.

"How are you, Hope?" Libby sat and Evan took the chair beside her.

Hope stared across the table at Libby without answering.

"I know it's got to be hard losing your good friend," Libby continued, "but I'm glad you're feeling better."

Met once again with silence, Libby let her sympathies go. "Thank you, Evan." She nodded toward her food.

"Are you shopping?" Evan asked.

"I just left work." Libby kept her gaze on Hope. The other woman squirmed under her scrutiny. What in the world was she doing? She needed to leave Hope alone. "How are you, Hope?" she repeated her earlier question.

"Hope's not doing too well today, Libby. Let's leave it at that," Evan answered.

"Oh," Libby took a deep breath. "I'm sorry. I can eat at another table, leave you two alone."

"Stay." Hope spoke for the first time, with the voice of someone else. Disdain always met Libby during their previous meetings. Now, Hope seemed almost resigned to accept her. Maybe she was being gracious. After all, she'd won the heart of the most wonderful man in the world. Libby lowered her head, trying to keep her emotions at bay.

"Libby, are you okay?" Evan leaned toward her.

"Yes." She pulled the paper from around her muffin.

"Do you mind if I thank the Lord for this food?" Evan held out his hands to both Libby and Hope.

Libby waited for Hope to take her lover's hand. Then she placed her hand against Evan's. His warmth closed over hers.

"Father, thank You for this food, and thank You for the lovely company I'm keeping today. In Jesus' name, Amen." Evan squeezed her hand and released it.

Libby kept her head bowed for a moment. Did Evan know what his words did to her heart? She absorbed every bit of his kindness, knowing she would have to wring it out later to simply survive without him. *Dear God, how much more do You want from me? My mother? My job? My heart? Take my apartment. I'm sick to death of the silence.*

She looked up to find them both staring at her.

She swallowed. "I received some bad news about my job. Sorry."

"So you really believe God hears a prayer from someone like you?" Hope crossed her arms over her chest.

Evan widened his eyes in Hope's direction. Even

Libby recognized the warning in his glare.

"Well, you too, Evan," Hope argued. "As if some God who operates heaven and makes the earth go around is going to care anything about the two of you."

"He cares a lot about you, and He's answered some pretty heavy prayers I sent up on your behalf." Evan drank his coffee. "Drink your smoothie, Hope. It's good for you."

Hope sat back in her chair as if Evan had slapped her. As she bounced against the hard seat, she raised her hand to the back of her head. For the first time, Libby noticed the gauze bandage wrapped around her head and tucked under the hat.

"Hope, what happened?" Libby looked from Hope to Evan. "Her head—"

Hope stared wide-eyed and then laughed. "You didn't tell her? Evan, that's rich."

"Evan, what happened to her? Did you …?"

Evan turned in his seat. "Did I what, Libby? Did I hurt Hope?"

"That's not what I was going to ask at all." Libby shot back at him. "I wanted to know …" Had Gideon and Charisse lied to her? Had Hope and Evan been involved in the accident that killed Tiffany?

Libby's heart lodged in her throat and then fell to her knees. His curt reply to her concern shattered her resolve and made her falter in her resolution not to run.

Evan looked away from her and back, his eyes searching her face.

"What difference does it make what I wanted to

know? You owe me no explanation. I thank God you're both safe." She turned her attention back to Hope. "Is there anything I can do?"

"What could you do?" Hope narrowed her eyes.

"I don't know. If you need to talk with someone, I'm available."

"Are you an expert on losing your best friend?" Hope challenged.

"Hope," Evan warned.

Darkness replaced the semi-friendliness Hope exhibited at first. "Do you know how it feels to lose someone you care about? Have you ever felt you could have done more to prevent what happened to them? What do you know about anything, Libby Overstreet? Yeah, I know your name now, but it doesn't matter. You have nothing for me."

Libby shot out of her seat. She fumbled in her purse and threw money onto the table. She would never take another thing from Evan Carter. "I didn't mean to upset you, but yes, Hope, I've faced grief. I'm glad you remember my name because if you ever need someone to talk to, I might be the one you'll want to come to for help. You and I aren't so different after all. I know how it feels to lose someone you love who loves you, and I know how it feels to love someone who hates you from the very depth of his soul." Her eyes met Evan's. If he wanted to chastise her for her rudeness, he'd better do it now. She'd never give him another chance.

She was ending her harmful fantasy today—this

moment.

Evan made no motion to smooth over the situation. He sat there without moving. She gave him another second to respond, but he remained motionless, mouth open, eyes wide.

"Please, enjoy the rest of your day. I need to go. There's someplace I need to be."

"Libby, I don't hate you." Evan finally found his voice. The scrape of his chair on the floor told her he'd moved after her. His touch on her arm stopped her at the door. "I can't believe you think I hate you. Libby. I—"

"I can't do this, Evan. Not now. Not ever." She rushed from the restaurant. She never thought he hated her. The problem was, he didn't love her either.

Evan hung his head as he walked back to the table. How could one person voice so much pain in so few words? Once again, he'd caused that pain, and he'd allowed Hope to add to it. With his hand on the back of his chair, he leaned forward and closed his eyes. "God, I can't do this. I place both of these women into Your hands."

"Sit down, Evan. You're making a scene."

He complied with Hope's demand.

She sighed and took a long sip of her smoothie. "Thank you."

"You have no idea what you've just done, do you?"

"She sits here and acts like she has the answers to all my problems. There's nothing she can do for me."

Evan brought his fist down on the table.

Hope jumped. She straightened and pushed away from the table.

Nate. Evan always knew a beating was coming when his father brought his fist down on something. It could be Evan; it could be a wall or a table.

Evan was not his father.

God, forgive me. "I'm sorry, Hope."

"What does she know about my life?"

If he didn't know any better, Evan would think she was fishing for an angry reaction from him. He wouldn't swallow her bait. "She's all alone. She has no family who cares for her."

Hope flinched. His well-chosen remark obviously hit home.

"Her mother is dead. She loved that woman very much. Mrs. Overstreet, from what I understand, was sick most of Libby's life. Libby dedicated herself to tending to her. Now, she's gone, and Libby has no one else."

"A father …?"

"All I know about her father is that he left her."

"But she didn't cause her mother to die. Tiffany—"

"You didn't kill Tiffany. I've told you that over and over again. Delilah has assured you Tiffany has gone home to be with the Lord. Grieve, Hope, but don't let your grief hurt others who only want to give you love and support."

"How can Libby offer me love? She doesn't even know me."

A genuine inquiry, not an argument. Evan fought the smile. "That's just it. Libby doesn't judge. That's another reason I love her. The thought of being hurtful horrifies her."

Hope played with the napkin on the table.

Evan looked to a clock hanging on the far wall. Time was ticking, and he was tired of the misunderstandings continuing to keep him away from Libby. "And now the woman I love thinks I hate her. How did she put it? She thinks I hate her from the very depth of my soul. The opposite is true. I love her with all I have."

At his words, Hope squirmed in her seat.

"Are you okay?" Evan asked.

Hope didn't lift her head with her gaze, but their eyes met just the same. "I'm sorry, Evan."

He tilted his head. This was a first. Hope Astor was apologizing for something, and with everything between them, he couldn't imagine what it was.

"You're a special man." She leaned forward, bending the straw in her cup back and forth. "And I used you. I've hurt you, and I've played with your affections. I've even stood between you and happiness."

And he'd used her as well, in an ugly way. He hadn't treasured her as a friend. He'd taken what she offered without any thought of the cost to her. Violence wasn't his only sin.

"It's always been Danny. I mean, you weren't hard on the eyes or anything, and I'd like to think we had some good times, that we could say we were friends. Friends with, you know how they're saying it these days, with benefits."

Evan shook his head. "The truth is that until the accident, I don't think we were friends, and what we shared weren't benefits. They came at a very expensive price. Our relationship was very inappropriate. You said it. We used each other.

"I want to be your friend, Hope, but I want to be your brother in Christ even more." Evan covered her hand with his. "We have a unique connection. Look at today. In just a matter of minutes, you have been my friend and my enemy. I don't like running from you. When you're being you, without the games, without the alcohol or drugs, I enjoy spending time together. There are things about our past I'd change if I could: my disrespect for you, taking from you what I shouldn't have taken. I can't change all of that, but our future, I hope as friends, is yet to be written." He swallowed hard and then leaned forward. "Forgive me for standing between you and Danny, too."

She waved her hand as if it didn't matter, but her lips trembled. "Danny forgot all about me. Left me behind. Can't blame him for that."

"He's hurting now, but give him awhile. Pray and let God work wonders."

She took a sip of her smoothie. "You can be so understanding, and I've made it difficult for you and Ms. Sunshine, haven't I?"

He smiled. "I think you've added to our difficulties,

but I'm new at this courtship thing." Heat crawled up his face as the next thought came to him. "Libby is so innocent and sweet. She's so vulnerable, and I was so good at getting my way with women ..."

"Yeah, you were." Hope actually laughed.

Evan didn't. "I'm beginning to see that all of this dancing around that we're doing may have been a good thing. She's so innocent and sweet, and even if she didn't love me, I'm flesh and blood, and she entices me so much. I could have gotten us into a lot of trouble."

"Evan, if we're going to be friends after today, I don't want to hear anymore."

He nodded. "As a friend, a true friend, would you do something for me?"

She didn't speak, only waited for him to continue. So like her. She didn't trust easily, and he'd never done anything for her to really gain faith in him.

"Libby needs someone. Even I can see she doesn't need me right now. Can I trust you to be there for her?" Evan took a deep breath and let it out. He was taking a tremendous risk here, but something deep inside told him these women needed each other. God had brought them together for a reason. Evan wasn't the only mutual friend of Hope's. Delilah cared for Libby and for Hope, and at times, he wondered if walking a fine line between both women wasn't wearing thin Delilah's patience with Hope. If he could only get Hope and Libby to see what they had in common. "What do you say, Hope?

"Yeah, right. You're going to trust me with her. She has her friend—Gideon's wife. What's her name?"

"Her name is Charisse, and she's as worried about Libby as Delilah and I are. Gideon's asked Charisse to hang back, and it's killing us to see Libby like this."

"And Charisse does everything her husband asks?" Hope smirked.

"Pretty much. If she doesn't agree with it, she talks it out with Gid. That's how marriage is supposed to work." Wasn't Libby's willingness to allow the Lord to lead her as a husband in her singleness one of the very attributes that deepened Evan's desire for her?

Hope shook her head. "Let's eat. Today is the last day you or Delilah has to babysit me. I'm clear to drive. I'm self-sufficient. Well, I am living on the goodness of Delilah, but you know what I mean."

"Will you try to talk to her for me?"

She leaned forward, drumming her fingernails on the table. "It's asking a lot, Evan, but you've been through the wringer for me the last few weeks." She pushed the cap down tighter on her head. "I'm terrible at making amends. Doing this for you will be my act of contrition. And if she's going to talk to me, guess I better make a list of the things I've done wrong so I can ditch my pride and make it a little easier to apologize." Hope dug into her purse. "Who would have thought when she gave me her card, I'd be using it to listen to her?"

"Maybe God?" Evan raised his brows.

"Yeah, right." Hope waved the card in the air as if to push the truth aside. "If I do this, I want one promise out of you."

So much for making amends. Her kind deed would come with a heavy price tag. "What is it?"

She smirked again. "When I work my magic, you move in and correct her thinking."

"Please don't share what I've said about my feelings for her. I'm not so sure I'm the one Libby needs. That's not why I'm asking you to do this."

"I know exactly why you're sending me out after her." She leaned back and crossed her arms over her chest. "You care about us both. We both care for you. You want us to be friends, and you think Libby can talk some God-sense into me." She waved the card again. "And, Evan, our wants and our needs, they're all the same. Go for it. She's yours for the taking."

Evan winced. Hope hadn't heard the sincerity in his voice when he'd apologized to her. He didn't want to take what didn't belong to him ever again. "God will provide my needs. When I pray for my desires, I have to wait on His answer. So far, I'm not sure of the direction He wants me to take."

"Seems pretty simple. You love her. I know she loves you. All you have to do is to see the way she looks at you."

Simple? His entire attempt at courtship with Libby had been one bumbling mistake after another. He had to love her. In the past, he would never continue to make a fool out of himself—not that he was doing this all alone. Gideon and Charisse had made some pretty disastrous moves all on their own, and Hope hadn't helped his cause. Still, he needed to make Hope understand. "Giving into my selfish desires can easily take Libby and me away from what God has for us. I'll wait."

But how long?

Dear God, either give me the desire of my heart or show me clearly Your desire for me. Please end this misery.

Chapter Sixteen

The forty-minute drive always seemed to take forever, but Libby found herself back in her hometown before she realized. She pulled into the driveway of Titusville's Oaklawn Memorial Gardens, drove down the narrow lane and onto a dirt path, parked, and picked up her Bible. Her steps crushed the dry oak leaves beneath her feet. The coolness of a light mist touched her skin, but she didn't care. Reading scripture at her mother's grave always calmed her. Even if the pages of her Bible got wet.

The family owning the plots beside her mother had furnished a bench. Libby sank to the damp concrete seat, sitting on the very corner. She reached out to touch the coldness of the granite etched with her mother's name, date of birth, and date of death. The information shared nothing of her mother's loving kindness and thoughtfulness, her dedication to the Lord, and her loving protection of her only child.

Unlike Tiffany's funeral, attendance had been small. Members of the small church she attended with her mother had stood beside her, and Gideon, Charisse, and Delilah had come together as members of Madge Overstreet's family. Each of them had grown to love Libby's ailing mother. They'd helped Libby care for her in those last few months when Madge could do very little and spent most of her time in the Orlando hospital.

Traffic whizzed by on the nearby street, but Libby gave them barely a notice. She longed to speak to her mother, but now the grave marker became a barrier between Libby and her mother's memory. More than anything, she wanted her mother beside her, her arms around her, Madge Overstreet telling her she was worthy of love and attention. No one else in Libby's life had ever given her the kind of love that built her up.

Charisse loved her. They were childhood friends, and they'd become closer over the last year. Libby thought of her as a sister, but no one ever compensated for her father's absence and his outright hatred like Momma had done.

Driving to Titusville indulged Libby's self-centered grief. In Hope's anger, Evan's lover had betrayed her pain. Libby had no right to think only of herself while Hope hurt so badly. "But I don't care, Lord. I don't care. Today, I'm thinking of myself. I refuse to think of Hope. I want You to be with her. I pray she finds peace. I beg You to find someone to talk to her, to show her You, but today, Father, I refuse." The light moisture dampened her hair, and she brushed the strands from her face.

The ringing phone startled her. She dug in her pocket and looked at the caller ID. Probably a wrong number. She flipped the phone open. "Yes, this is Libby."

"Libby, this is Hope."

Libby pursed her lips and looked toward heaven. Why wouldn't God allow her one more ounce of self-pity today?

"Are you there?"

"How did you get my number?" Libby curled her fingers around the edge of the bench and squeezed.

"You gave me your card in the coffee shop."

So she had no one else to blame for this interruption of her time.

"What can I do for you?" She cleared her throat, the harshness of her reply surprising even her. She straightened, not willing to relinquish the tone quite yet.

"Could you meet with me?"

"Why?" Libby leaned forward, her spine straight. Nothing boded well in Hope's sweet tone. The woman was setting a trap. Libby was sure. She probably wanted to warn Libby to stay away from Evan. Hope needn't worry. She planned to stay as far away from the man as possible.

"Well, you said you would talk to me, and you know what I'm going through. Right now, I need someone who cares about me."

Libby gasped at Hope's admission. "And you think I do?" After the words left her mouth, Libby nearly bit her tongue. From where had this dangerously bitter attitude sprung? "I apologize, Hope. I do care."

"So, you'll talk to me. I'll come to where you are."

"I'm at the Oaklawn Cemetery in Titusville."

A pause, an awkward moment fell between them. "When will you be home?" Hope asked.

"Later." Much later.

Hope hesitated. "I can wait until you get back. Maybe

we can meet for dinner."

The weariness set in. Hope obviously wanted Libby on her own turf. "May I ask you one question?"

"Yes."

"What happened to your head? I mean why do you have a bandage around your head?"

Silence again stretched between them.

"Hope?"

"I talked Tiffany into partying with me. I got hurt in a bar. Maybe someone pushed me. I don't know. Cut my head wide open. I didn't know I was injured. That's how drunk I was. I had Tiffany drop me off at Evan's house."

The night she'd been on the phone with Evan, Hope had been at his door.

"I almost died," Hope continued. "Evan got me to the hospital. Libby, Tiffany wrecked her car after she left me with Evan. She died in the same emergency room. And I lived."

And nearly losing Hope, Evan realized how much he loved her.

Libby lifted her eyes toward heaven. Didn't Charisse tell her God was always in the details? And He was, even if those details broke Libby's heart. God had something better for her, although she could think of no one better than Evan. And Evan was involved with a woman who didn't know the Lord. If Libby truly loved the man, she'd want the best for him.

Okay, Lord. I understand.

"Libby, why are you at the cemetery?"

"I sometimes come here and sit by my mother's

grave to talk to the Lord. I miss her." Libby's voice trembled. "And I miss the times we prayed together and talked. This is my way of dealing with losing her."

"Will you meet me?"

How do you tell someone you don't trust her? And I don't trust her, Lord. Not yet. I need her to prove herself to me. Libby took a deep breath and let it out before speaking. "I don't trust you, Hope. It's that plain and simple, but I'll take a chance on you hurting me because I do care for you." Well, that would do it. *Thank you, Lord.*

Hope's sigh met Libby's ears. "I deserve that."

"It's okay," Libby said. "I haven't been kind to you at times, and I apologize."

Now Hope laughed. "Evan knows you so well. It's like you two were meant for each other."

Libby closed her eyes. Was Hope trying to be deliberately cruel?

"I'll meet you wherever you say," Hope said.

She'd have to take the chance. She told Hope she would. "My address is on my card. Meet me there around seven. I'll cook us some dinner."

"No. No, don't do that. I'll bring us something to eat."

"Are you okay to drive? I'm sorry. I didn't think of that."

"Yes, the doctor cleared me this morning, and Evan and Delilah have let me out from under their watchful care."

Delilah had known about Evan and Hope. The

betrayal threatened to cave in Libby's heart. She cleared her throat. God had arranged this. Libby was sure of it. Delilah had Libby's best interest in mind. "I'll see you then."

Libby stared at her mother's name on the cold granite. A chill caused by the misty rain ran down her spine. "Your daughter is a fool, Momma, and so inept with handling anything in this life without you."

She bowed her head. Momma wasn't listening. She was in heaven where problems ceased. Momma was living without the burdens of illness. Even if she could hear her daughter's cries, she'd probably have only one bit of advice, "Libby, sweetheart, none of it will matter when you come home."

"Oh, Heavenly Father, I'm so sorry. I told You what I would do, and I didn't ask what You would have from me. Forgive me for my self-centered nature today. Keep me from feeling sorry for myself, and ever be my reminder that I am never alone when I have You."

Libby used the bench now as an altar. Bending on her knees, she began to pray for Hope and for the words the Lord would have for her to get through to this woman so lost in self-centeredness herself. "I need your protection, Father. Evan is right. I am out of Hope's league."

Evan found himself at the nursing home. Why he'd given up the invitation to a nice dinner with the guys—Gideon and his son, V.J.—was beyond him, but he wanted to keep to the plan he'd laid out for Gideon during their earlier phone conversation. He needed to talk to his father, get beyond the disabling bitterness. Until he did that, he didn't deserve Libby.

Gideon had prayed with Evan over the phone. He could do this.

"Mr. Carter, I don't think you want to see your father right now. He's had a very rough day." An aide breezed past.

He stopped with his hand still on the door of Nate's room. A bad day for Nate meant worse for Evan if he dared approach. Standing in the middle of the hallway, he watched the elderly residents of the nursing home going about their day. Some sat in very uncomfortable looking chairs by the nurses' station unaware of the world passing them by, but many remained a part of this world. Nate was losing his grasp on reality, leaving his sons in the nightmare world he'd made for them.

Before Evan could laugh at the bitter irony, he felt a grasp on his arm. He turned and looked into the eyes of an elderly woman in a wheelchair. Her hands trembled as she held on to him. "You've come to visit me, haven't you? I haven't had a visitor today."

Evan started to shake his head, but he saw the desire for companionship in the woman's eyes. When so many ran from the sadness of this place, Libby lived to touch lives like this one. Hadn't Libby touched him in this place as well?

"Yes, ma'am, I'd love to visit with you. How did you

know? Why don't we go into the recreation room and sit for a while?"

A smile beamed across the wrinkled face as Evan pushed her wheelchair into the empty room. He parked her chair and sat in front of her. "I'm Evan."

"Scarlet," she blushed.

"As in O'Hara?"

"Exactly," her body trembled from age or disease, but her smile was bright. "My father used to call me Scarlet Katie."

Evan laughed aloud until he noticed the look of confusion on the woman's face—or was it a hint of amusement. "Scarlet Katie O'Hara," he said in his best Irish brogue.

"Oh, you knew my father?"

Evan nodded. "Well, Scarlet Katie, how are you today?"

"I'm better now that I have a visitor."

"Do you have friends here?"

She nodded. "But they have family, and mine are gone."

"I'm sorry to hear that, Scarlet."

"I've seen you here before. You come to visit Nate Carter."

Evan nodded. "He's my father."

"Your father is very lucky to have a son like you."

Evan winced. He hadn't been very lucky to have a father like Nate.

"A father's inheritance always shows up in the nature of his son."

"I hope not." Sarcasm slipped out with his words.

Scarlet touched his arm. "But not always in the way you think." She held up a boney finger as if to correct him. "Sometimes a weak father makes a strong son. The boy has to make up for the weaknesses of his dad."

"My father wasn't weak, Scarlet. He was very strong."

She searched his face, and he wondered if she could see into his soul. "A bad father can birth a very good son. Overbearing evil sometimes has a way of producing goodness in others. Like oppression has a way of making people fight for freedom."

How could she know? Evan covered the hand Scarlet left on his arm. "You are one smart lady."

"Experienced is all."

"You must know the Lord to have all that knowledge."

Scarlet studied him as if weighing something. Then she looked beyond him. "I don't have much time for all that nonsense."

"Scarlet, Scarlet, Scarlet." Evan leaned close. "Since you've shared some of your knowledge with me, may I share some wisdom with you?"

She scrunched her nose and again seemed to weigh his words. After a few moments, she smiled. "Love to hear it." She moved her wheelchair toward him, bending forward, as if she thought Evan might hold the answers to all life's riddles.

And by God's grace, he did.

Chapter Seventeen

Libby fumbled in her purse for the keys to her apartment. As she jingled them in her hand, her mobile rang. She slipped a key in her lock and searched for the phone. Charisse's number showed up on the screen.

She put the phone to her ear and opened her door. "Charisse." She pulled out the keys and threw them on the counter. "Are you there?" She pushed the door shut.

"Yes. Are you home?"

"Just arrived. I went to Titusville to talk to Momma." She sat on the couch and took off her shoes, though Hope would arrive at any minute, unless she'd changed her mind.

"And how is Madge?" Charisse asked.

"She was busy enjoying heaven, so I ended up talking with God instead."

Charisse laughed "Ah, there's the Libby I've missed. Listen, are you up for company?"

"I'm expecting someone in a few minutes. Why?"

"Oh, the boys are enjoying a Three Stooges marathon, and you know those make me cringe. They plan to stay up all night watching them. The challenge is to see if they can both remain awake through church tomorrow."

"And you're going to let them both get away with

it—the big kid and the little kid?"

Charisse laughed. "You and I know they'll both be asleep on the couch by ten o'clock. I wondered if we could do a slumber party tonight. You know, eat all the stuff that's bad for us, watch a chick-flick, make fun of each other, and laugh about our childhoods. See if we can stay awake through church tomorrow …"

Libby wanted to do that more than anything in the world. She'd lifted prayers to God about her loneliness and her desire for companionship. While she might have pictured Evan as her companion, God had other plans. Evan loved another, and she needed to deal with the truth of it.

"Lib?"

"Yeah?" She looked at her clock hanging on the wall. "My visitor should be here anytime now. Can you come over around eight?" By then, if Hope planned to attack her, Libby would need Charisse's shoulder to cry on.

"Nope, I'm here already. Will you open the door?"

"What?" Libby laughed.

"Open your door."

"What are you up to?"

"We're outside."

Libby ran to the door and pulled it open. "*We? * What in the world?"

Charisse and Delilah stood with bags of groceries in their hands.

Libby jumped up and down like a child receiving a big surprise. "What do you have?" She pulled them inside then stood face to face with Hope, still wearing her baseball cap and carrying more bags. "Let me take those." Libby grabbed them from her. "Come in. What a surprise."

"Libby, this is all Hope's idea." Charisse went into the kitchen. "Delilah and I brought all the junk food to give you zits and cellulite, but Hope, well, you tell her."

"She wants to make you all beautiful," Delilah explained instead.

Libby stared from one to the other. "Oh." What else could she say? She always knew she wasn't the loveliest thing in the world, but she didn't expect Charisse and Delilah to allow someone to point it out to her.

"Thank you, Delilah." Hope narrowed her eyes in Delilah's direction.

"No problem." Delilah pushed Charisse into the kitchen. "Let's get all the goodies out."

"Libby, that's not what I told them." Hope glared toward the kitchen.

"I'm that hideous, huh?" Libby asked the woman who'd won Evan's heart.

Hope tilted her head and then touched her hand to the bandage with a wince. "It still hurts when I do that," she said.

"Why don't you sit down?" Libby led Hope into her small living room.

"Nice place," Hope said, but her face told Libby the truth.

She would not apologize. God had been good to allow her to find this apartment, and Libby decided just this afternoon that she should never again be discontent with what God gave to her. She was still working on being content without what God chose to keep from her.

"You wanted to talk. We can go into my room. I'll tell Charisse and Delilah we'll be with them soon."

Hope shook her head. "Maybe later. With what I've already said to you and about you, I don't expect you to believe me, but Delilah took my words out of context."

Libby flipped her drab hair upward. "It's no secret. I'm not a beauty."

Hope touched Libby's hair. "Have you ever thought of darkening the brown a bit?"

"I've never given much thought to it."

"Can I be honest with you?" Hope asked as Delilah and Charisse came into the room loaded down with trays and bags of goodies. They set them around the room.

"Slumber down!" Charisse squealed and plopped into Libby's overlarge chair on the other side of the room. "Like we used to do, Lib. Won't this be fun?"

Libby nodded but gave Hope her full attention. "Go ahead."

"When I first met you, I did say some ugly things about your looks. I even told Evan you were a hideous creature."

Charisse scrambled to her feet, but Delilah stood, holding Charisse away with the palm of her hand.

"But, Libby, I was wrong." With her finger under Libby's chin, Hope tipped Libby's face and stared. "My artist eye sees untapped beauty—beauty Evan could see with his own eye for artistry, but until this afternoon in Java Lava, it was hidden from me."

Libby pulled from Hope's touch. "Can we not talk about Evan?"

"Sure." Hope reached and slipped off Libby's glasses. "Look at Charisse and Delilah."

Libby hesitated but did as Hope asked, looking at her friends through squinty eyes. "With her green eyes, what do you girls think about a little darker color on her hair?"

"Yeah, and a little less brow?" Delilah laughed. "Libby, do you ever pluck your eyebrows?"

"Once a week, but I can't shape them."

"Obviously," Delilah said, and Charisse elbowed her.

Libby stuck out her tongue at Delilah.

"I have a friend who owns a salon. She went with me this afternoon to get the perfect salon color for you—not one of those you buy at the grocery store. I know how to do this. I bought the color, the makeup, the eyebrow wax, the nail polish, some makeup. Well, Delilah did loan me the money," Hope said.

"I don't know." Libby looked at Charisse.

"She doesn't trust me," Hope announced. "She told me so. That's why I asked you ladies to join me. On my honor, I only want Libby to see the beauty in herself."

"Libby is beautiful." Charisse placed her hands on her hips.

"Yes, you are." Hope smiled at Libby. "You just haven't worn your beauty so everyone can see it on the outside."

"Why are you doing this for me?"

"Because I lost one of my best friends, and Evan tells me you'd be a wonderful one. Not to replace Tiffany, but to help me forget, at least for a bit." Hope stood. "You've been nice to me since the day we met, and I've been horrible to you. If you knew half of the problems I've caused, you'd tell me to leave your apartment right now. This is my way of apologizing."

Libby rose and enfolded Hope in a hug. "You could simply say you're sorry. Take these things back, and repay Delilah. She's pretty cheap, you know."

Delilah uttered a fake gasp. "Well, I never. Who bought our last lunch?"

"I did," Charisse declared.

"Well, cheap and stupid are polar opposites. You pulled out the debit card first. Who am I to balk?"

"I'll have to remember that for our next girl's night out. I wondered why I always paid."

Delilah clamped her lips together as if she'd let a secret she never wanted to let out of the bag of brashness she carried around.

Hope laughed then sobered. "I want to do this. Will you let me?" She wiped teary eyes.

"You do the hair." Delilah pointed. "I'll do the makeup, and Charisse can do her nails."

Libby stood and raised her hands in surrender. "I don't think I have a choice. Do what you will."

The world had gone haywire. The woman Evan loved was trying to make her beautiful. For whom, another man?

There would never be another.

Evan had never spent much time with any of the residents of the nursing home, and he began to see why Libby loved to minister here.

Scarlet Katie O'Hara laughed as she and Evan raised their heads from her prayer for salvation. "And you think you've got your daddy's badness. Not when you shed a tear over something like this."

With the back of his hand, Evan wiped the embarrassing tears from his eyes. "I think God used you today to show me a few truths, Scarlet Katie O'Hara."

Scarlet laughed. "Just so you don't go away thinking I'm an old lunatic, my first name is Scarlet, but my middle name is Renee, and my last name is Trevetti, not O'Hara. I'm Italian, not Irish."

Evan blinked. "Deputy Trevetti?"

Scarlet lowered her head. "I didn't think you'd remember."

Evan stood and paced the room. This woman, an older deputy, had often been to Evan's childhood home, called by the neighbors who did nothing else.

Her name tag had been pinned to her uniform. With every call to his home, he had hope, but his mother never told the truth.

Before his mother had died she'd asked his forgiveness, said fear kept her married to Nate for so long, kept her from telling the truth. She had to wait until all her boys were gone before she could leave because if Nate caught up with her, he would only take her life away from her.

Evan understood her fear.

"I'm sorry, Evan," Scarlet said from behind him. "I told Libby that if I ever got the chance to talk to you, that I'd never embarrass you. Seems I did just that."

"Libby?" He spun toward the older woman. "What did you tell her?" He sat back beside her.

"She wouldn't let me tell her much. She's not one for gossip, but Evan I know she loves you. I half-jokingly told her that if I got the chance to talk to you, it would be God's proof of His existence for me." She looked up at him. "What can I do to make it up to you?"

Evan smiled. "I think you need to repent right way." He touched her hand. "I thank you for the wisdom you shared. The repentance is for fooling me. I really thought you were suffering from dementia, and you really thought you were Scarlet O'Hara."

She gave a hearty laugh. "Sometimes you young ones need to know us old ones are still sharp witted."

"Well, Scarlet, may I walk you to your room?"

"No. You go visit your daddy."

"The nurse told me he's had a bad day." Evan picked at a callous on his hand.

"Better you see him then. Don't you think?"

He thought for a second and then nodded in agreement. He'd ignored Nate for too long. He needed to start the road to healing.

"You'll come back to see me?" She peered at him with hopeful eyes.

"Soon," he promised. "Very soon."

"I'll be looking for you. I want you to bring Libby with you the next time. You can't hide your feelings from me any more than she can. I knew the moment I saw you two in the chapel that day, you were in love with her. She loves you, too, and she's been sad lately. If you had anything to do with that, you'll answer to me. I adore that little gal."

"Scarlet, you're right. I do love that *little gal*, but I hurt her every time I see her."

"Now, how can that be?" Scarlet reached a trembling hand toward him.

Evan held her hand in his. "I can't tell you, but there's something in me that harms her each time we're together."

"Have you told her how you feel?"

"When I believe she fully understands how madly in love with her I am, she'll say something or do something that makes me think she hasn't a clue."

"Men." Scarlet shook her head. "Listen to me. You need to tell that gal tonight. Spell it out for her. A woman hears with her heart, not with her ears. That heart can't hear over the noise of you fellows stumbling and fumbling, thinking you've made it clear. Make it obvious. 'Libby, I love you.' It's that simple."

Evan squeezed Scarlet's hand. Spell it out. Libby herself told him how inexperienced she was at love. He had been awkward and uncertain around her, afraid to allow Libby to love him because he feared what he could do to her in the wake of his too-well experienced life. Yet, he'd hung around, trying to make her see that he did cherish her, wanting a chance to prove it to her. As he'd told Hope, the dancing around might have been a good protection for Libby, but no wonder she was so confused. "I'll do that, Scarlet. I promise."

"And you'll bring her with you the next time to prove it to me." Hers was a demand, not a question.

He nodded. "Yes, ma'am."

"Then get along and see that daddy of yours."

Evan waved as he left, heading toward Nate's room. He caught a nurse's eye, nodded, and entered.

Nate lay in the bed, both rails up for his safety. He appeared weak and old, reminding Evan of Scarlet's words. Nate stared out the window seemingly unaware of Evan's presence. Evan moved cautiously to the only chair in the room and sat.

Nate's fingers pinched at the white sheets, but other than that, he remained calm.

Evan studied his father's face. Long ago, someone noted all of Nate's sons bore a resemblance to their mother. Yet all had the scars given to them by their father.

As Evan continued to watch, emotion welled within him. The fact anger wasn't a part of it surprised him. "Dad, I'll be a legacy you don't deserve. By me, I'll give you a good name. What you've done doesn't matter. I am not what you tried to make me. Your violence and your hatred allowed God to instill kindness and love in me. I have to have faith."

"What are you doing here?" Nate's gruff voice met Evan's declaration.

Evan didn't flinch. "I've come to see you."

Nate grumbled and continued to look out the window.

"Dad, do you know who I am?"

"You're the son that woman gave me. The only good thing she gave me."

"You have four sons." Evan stood and held to the bars on the bed keeping Nate in place.

"But you were the one I couldn't break. You're the strong one."

His father had never given him any encouragement. In fact, Nate had branded him a coward with the hot poker to Evan's skin.

But Evan had to let it go. He had to heal this relationship, and the forgiveness had to come from him.

"Did you ever think love could make us all strong? Love could have saved Momma from the life you put her through."

"What do I know of love, boy? Nothing. How could I teach you?"

"Did your dad beat you?"

"My dad. My mom. I was a punching bag. I never got no love. How could I give it to you? No one ever loved me."

"Why do you think I took you into my home until you got too violent for the nurses there? Why do you think I'm here now?" Evan asked.

"They make you come."

"No. The only thing they make me do is pay the bill."

Nate laughed. "That's a big bill, ain't it?"

"I don't much notice. I know you're safe here."

Nate's eyes widened and then narrowed. "Why would you care about me?"

Evan took a deep breath. *Why, Lord? Why should I care about him?* He stared out the window for a long moment, waiting for the Lord's answer. God's reply came with peace that relaxed Evan's tense shoulder and filled him with a calm he'd never experienced around his father.

He leaned down so his father could see him clearly. "I care about you because God gave me my heritage. Because of that, I'm where I am now. God molded the good and the bad from both you and Momma, and I'm who I am today because of it. I'm God's child because God directed my paths even in the midst of the nightmares you created."

"So, you're thanking me for what I put you through?"

"I'm thanking my heavenly Father for the fire that burned away the dross. He brought me through it. The beginning and the middle might not be what I would have chosen for myself, but where I am today makes it all worthwhile."

Nate didn't speak for a moment. Then he swallowed hard. "I haven't seen that angel who used to visit me before. Have you seen her, boy? She's the one with the funny big glasses and the sweet face." Father and son stared at one another. So, Nate truly didn't remember what he'd done to Libby, and Libby didn't hold Nate's actions against him, Evan needed to let that go as well.

"She's my angel, Nate. And if God gives me the chance I'm praying for, I'll bring her back to visit you."

Nate turned his gaze back to the window, and Evan walked away. "Lord, you've opened the door. Please keep it open for me." He said the prayer as he entered the hall. "And maybe the next one I'm about to barge through, too."

Outside the nursing home, he dialed Libby's number.

"Hello, Libby's Playhouse and Beauty Salon," a giggling voice greeted him.

"Libby?" He smiled.

"Evan?" Libby said. "Are you calling for Hope?"

His smile vanished. "Why would I call your place looking for her?"

"Because she's here, and she's staying overnight. Didn't she tell you?"

Ah, no. If Hope had told him this was part of her plan, he would have panicked way before now. Hope was capable of playacting too well. A whole evening with Libby could start out friendly and turn pretty ugly. "Libby, be careful. Hope can hurt you worse than I ever have."

"Evan," Libby lowered her voice. "What a horrible thing to say about the woman you said you love."

When had he said he loved Hope? He loved Libby.

"Let me get her for you."

"Wait, Libby." He turned in a complete circle

looking to the heavens and casting a silent "Why?" in God's direction.

"Hello?" Hope answered.

"Hope, what are you doing there? Please tell me you're not going to hurt her."

"I'm doing what you asked me to do. We're having a good time. Charisse and Delilah are here, too."

"I'm in the twilight zone. Tell me why you have to stay the night?"

"You'll see soon enough. Did you need me?" she asked.

"No, I want to speak to Libby."

"Well, she's busy now. You have a great evening. I hear Gideon Tabor is having a Three Stooges marathon at his place. Go join him."

Click.

And that was the end of his call.

What had he done? He'd created another fiasco, and this might be the one to turn his dreams into an endless nightmare.

Hope was with Libby, and when Hope got through with her, Libby would never want him around her again.

Chapter Eighteen

Libby's eyebrows were waxed, her hair dyed, shampooed, and conditioned with expensive salon purchases. With a towel wrapped securely around her hair, Hope had sent her out to Charisse and Delilah who simultaneously gave her a manicure and applied makeup. Now, she was back in the bathroom sitting in a chair with her back to the mirror, her wet hair falling to the floor with each snip of Hope's scissors.

"Libby, do you really find comfort from a patch of ground where a bunch of old bones are buried?" Hope asked.

Libby nodded, and Hope put her hands on each side of Libby's face. "Hold still."

"I find comfort in knowing even though her bones are in the ground her soul is with Jesus where I'll meet up with her again someday."

Hope stopped her work.

"Do you have that expectation, Hope?"

"What expectation?" Hope lifted a handful of Libby's thick hair, pinned it to the top of her head, and continued to clip away.

"Do you expect to see Tiffany in heaven someday?"

"No, I guess I don't."

"Because you don't know if she's there?"

Hope stopped her cutting and came around in front of Libby. She leaned against the bathroom door. "Well, Delilah said she is, but how do I know?"

"Oh, Hope, I know she's there now. Remember the day I followed you out of Java Lava, and I gave you my card? When we left, we missed something precious. God used Delilah to introduce Himself to Tiffany, and she trusted in Him."

"But she went out with me that night, and she died. I shamed her into going. How could she be in heaven when we were both drunk?"

"Because God is perfect and merciful. His children are imperfect. We need His mercy. Christ dying on the cross was his ultimate compassion toward us. He gave so much—His only Son—so you and I can have a relationship with Him despite our imperfections."

Hope leaned her head against the door and winced. "How long has your mother been gone? Evan said she was your only relative. What about your dad?"

Libby fought the urge to push the subject Hope avoided. "Oh, I have cousins, but they don't live close. Mom's been gone nearly a year now. She was sick for a long time though. And my earthly father, he's around somewhere. He doesn't want anything to do with me."

"I know how that feels. My parents washed their hands of me." Hope pushed away from the door and resumed her clipping. "My mom is using this as a life lesson. She wants me to give up my passion, to settle down, go to college, and get a degree. If I bow to her every whim, I can come back home."

"I'm sorry," Libby whispered. She'd been lucky. Her mother expected Libby to do what made her happy. While her mom was alive, she had been Libby's focus. "I threw my mother's dreams for me away," she said more to herself. "I'm sorry that your mom doesn't understand your desires, but you know, she must love you to want you to make something of your life."

"My daddy loves me," Hope said without much emotion. "But Mom—she's like a machine, and Daddy is kind of tied to her. He does what she says."

Libby's heart ached for that family. God never intended for a woman to lead a household. Even in her household of one, Libby liked knowing that the man of her home was Jesus. She tried to look to Him for everything.

Hope continued to shape Libby's hair. At least that's what Libby assumed. For all she knew, Hope could be butchering the cut.

"You know your mother's in heaven? You're sure of this?" Hope finally asked.

"Yeah, we both trusted in Him when I was fourteen."

"I don't understand it. Delilah used to be as hateful toward people like you as I've been. I've seen a change in her, and I don't understand how she could go from being so angry at someone for the things you believe to defending you with passion. And she and Evan have been so good to me since the accident even though I've been hateful toward both of them."

Libby reached to still Hope's hands. Hope placed the

scissors on the sink, and Libby looked down at all the hair on her floor wondering if she had any left.

She'd let Hope shave her bald if the woman would only grasp what she had to say.

"Christ calls people to Him in different ways. I don't know exactly why Delilah finally accepted His outstretched arms, but I looked to Christ because I needed a Father who would love me. Oh, God knew I needed Him in so many other ways, but my earthly father's absence was the pain I needed quelled in my life."

Hope sat on the closed lid of the toilet and bent forward, her arms crossed over her stomach.

Libby's heart raced. Maybe Hope was ready to listen. "All our needs are special, but they are met in Christ. When I was two years old, my father walked out on my mother and me. He bounced in and out of our lives until I was about five. I'm the reason he walked away permanently. Momma was proud, and she worked hard to keep our house and to raise me. When she got ill, we struggled. The sicker she became, the bigger and stronger the roots of bitterness began to grow inside her. Then one day a friend invited me to church, and I went. When I got home, I explained to Momma how the preacher told me about Someone who loved me no matter what—Someone I could call Father, Someone who could give her a gift so precious her sickness would mean so little.

"The next week, Momma went to church, and she and I met Jesus for the first time. She told me then she held on to the bitterness not because of what my dad had done to her, but for what he'd done to me. When I told her about God and how He wanted to be the Father I never had, her bitterness melted away."

"But He didn't remove her sickness or bring your father back to you?"

"No, He didn't, but in taking away Momma's resentment, He gave us both better days to enjoy together until He called her home. Momma had hope of a better life away from here, and she knew when she left I'd never be alone. I have a Father to care for me. My earthly father was only the man through whom God gave me life."

"So why didn't she just kill herself and move on to that world?" Hope, her arms still across her stomach, rocked her body back and forth. "I want to, Libby. I don't want to be here any longer. I haven't wanted to be here for a very long time."

Libby gasped. "Oh, Hope, God has a much more wonderful plan for us while we're still here. Trust in Him, and trust Him to see you through this. Your pain, your problems, they're part of life. And if you trust Him, they may not be taken away from you, but you'll have Him to lean upon." She brushed Hope's hair from her wet cheeks. "Besides, we don't trust Him to avoid life. He has a purpose for us, work to do, people to tell about His goodness and the *hope* He offers to us, Hope."

Hope stopped her rocking and turned her head to look at Libby. "People like me?"

"Now, do you see why Delilah and Evan have changed, why they've tried to get you to see there's a better life? They have a promise. When their work is done here, they have a home on the other side. But on this side, they have a purpose. For both of them, you are part of that purpose. They love you very much."

"When I woke up in the hospital, I heard Evan praying for me."

Libby swallowed her pride and her pain with a big gulp. Of course, Evan would pray. He was a wonderful Christian man. "Evan loves you. I know he does."

Hope resumed her rocking. "Libby, when I went drinking with Tiffany, she tried to talk to me about this Christianity thing. I laughed at her because she got all tongue tied, and because the possibility of losing another friend to God sickened me. I thought having a few drinks and swallowing a pill or two would take away my sadness. Drinking only made it worse, and it made me more determined to bring Evan down with me. I planned to seduce him. Getting him to make love to me used to be so easy."

Libby closed her eyes, not wanting to see the picture of Evan and Hope that the woman was painting for her. How could she reconcile the Evan Hope described with the man who'd treated her with such respect? Was Hope being deliberately cruel?

"The honest truth is that Evan fed something in me that made me feel alive. When he was drinking, he was fun to be around unless he was in a bad mood. Then watch out. But it was that swing in his moods that exhilarated me. It kept my mind off of the man I really loved."

"Yes, alcohol hides the real man. I'm so glad he

doesn't drink any longer. He's a good man, Hope. Such a good man."

Hope met Libby's tear-filled gaze with her own and half laughed, half cried. "Look at you, so devastated for me after the way I've treated you." Hope's choking sobs tore at Libby's heart.

"Did he ever hit you, Hope? Evan? Was he ever physically abusive with you?"

Hope shook her head. "He usually took his anger out at anyone who slighted him. I saw what he could do. I didn't go there. I stayed by his side. I usually egged him on to get him to fight." She looked to the ceiling. "Funny thing is, I've done more to agitate him since he became a Christian, trying to prove it was just a phase. He gets frustrated with me now, but never truly angry."

"But you—you've been with him."

Hope stared at Libby for a long moment. "Do you want the truth?"

Libby nodded. "I know I have no reason to ask. It's none of my business."

"It's every bit of your business, but I want you to know that it was before. I don't want you to think Evan has done anything since—you know—since he became a Christian. The boy has practically been a monk since the accident that sobered him up for good."

Libby nodded. Evan had been lost and hurting before the Lord changed his heart. With her, he'd been nothing but a gentleman. He'd respected her, and that's why she'd let herself believe he could cherish her the way she'd prayed and asked God to allow Evan to do.

She wouldn't hold his past against him. To do so, would be to say that God hadn't done enough. And God had forgiven Evan. How could she not see beyond his past to see what Evan had now become?

"Libby?" Hope straightened. She shook her head as if shrugging off a shroud of pain, and then she slumped forward. "Tiffany's dead. Evan tells me he's partly to blame. That's not true. I'm the reason she's gone. Not him. Everyone's told me Tiffany's in heaven, but I can't let go of this sadness." Hope stared at the floor.

Libby remained silent, waiting for Hope to look at her. When she did, Libby's heart wrenched from the pain etched on Hope's face. "What made you so angry about Tiffany's Christianity?"

"I don't know," Hope said. "I can't put my finger on it."

"Maybe you felt you had no one to go out and party with?"

"Maybe."

"Or is it you can't understand what would make her want to abandon such a fun lifestyle that leaves you with stitches in your skull?"

"Yeah, that was fun, all right." A glimmer of a smile showed on Hope's face.

"That lifestyle isn't fun anymore, is it? You know you need something better than a temporary fix for sadness or loneliness. Maybe, like Evan has done, you need to allow this accident to change your course in life. You've seen Delilah smile and call Charisse and me her sisters. You've seen Evan's rage evaporate. Look at us here tonight. We've been laughing and giggling without one drop of alcohol."

"But a ton of ice cream and candy bars and chips and dip." A true smile turned the corners of Hope's lips then faded. "How did it happen? How did they change? Libby, if you'd known Evan before, you'd have avoided him as much as you should have avoided me."

Libby didn't want to talk about Evan. He was Hope's now, not hers. And she had more important things to discuss with the woman Evan loved.

"Jesus." Libby allowed the truth of His Name to seep into Hope's obviously softening soul. "Only Jesus and His mercy can fill the void you have in your life. Jesus' love changes us. He changed me. He changed Delilah. He changed Evan, and He can change you."

"Mercy? Is that the word you used? I could stand to have a bit of that in my life. How do I get God to be merciful toward me after all I've done?"

"Tell Him what you need. He wants to hear you tell Him you know what your life has been without Him. Ask God to forgive you, and ask Jesus to love you. He never refuses those requests."

Hope lifted the baseball cap gingerly from her head. A long scar with hair barely growing back made Libby gasp. "Honey, you're lucky to be alive. Thank Him for giving you this chance to know Him."

"What can I bring to Him?"

"The only thing you have is your brokenness. Give it

to Him, not in exchange for His love, but so He can replace your sorrow for joy. Let me get my Bible. I can show you."

"No." Hope jumped to her feet.

Libby's heart fell.

"I don't want them to see the finished product until we're done. I'll get it. Where is it?"

A knock sounded, and the door opened slightly. Delilah pushed a Bible through the crack.

Libby laughed. "No eavesdropping, you two."

Hope stared at the Bible in her hand before handing it to Libby.

Libby leafed through the pages. "Here let me show you."

"I didn't come here for this. I came to make you the most beautiful woman in the world."

Libby smiled. "Well, if you do that, we'll surely witness a miracle, but let's follow God's plans for a few minutes. Evan will be so thrilled if your heart wraps itself in God's truth."

Hope touched the open Bible page. "Evan doesn't hate you, Libby. He loves you very much."

Libby turned the pages of her Bible without looking up. "I know he doesn't hate me. Where did you ever get that idea?" She found her place in the book of Romans. "Let's start here."

"He thinks you do. He thought that's what you meant when you left us at Java Lava. He's torn up about it."

"Let's not worry about Evan and me. There's a greater love waiting for you, and I want to share it. Let's start at Romans 3:10."

Evan waited in Gideon's family room. In front of him, the Three Stooges bonked, hit, and scratched. He couldn't even smile at their silly antics.

Gideon thundered down the stairs and leaned into the room. "Want something to drink?"

"No. Sorry I interrupted your time with V.J."

Gideon bounced down on the couch. "He fell asleep an hour ago." He picked up the remote and clicked off the television. "And I was sitting here missing my wife."

"She's with Libby?"

"Yeah. They're having a slumber party. Now, let me try that one out on her, 'Charisse, dear, some of the guys are coming over to spend the night.'" Gideon laughed. "I can understand why Delilah and Charisse are at Libby's, but why is Hope with them?"

"I sent her." Evan looked to the ceiling wishing he could go back in time to Java Lava and undo everything he'd placed in motion. When would he ever get anything right when it came to dealing with Libby? "How'd you know Hope was with them?"

"They were all over here packing up food from the pantry and stealing my ice cream. I heard Hope say something about a makeover."

Evan cut his gaze to Gideon. "Makeover?"

"Yeah, another one of those girly things. Maybe I'll

try that one on Charisse next weekend. 'Honey, Evan and I are getting together with a few friends for a makeover. Can I use your eye shadow?'" Gideon batted his eyes and puckered his lips.

Evan shook his head at his friend's antics, but he was in no mood to laugh. "Why would four beautiful women want to ruin their looks with makeup?"

Gideon studied Evan for a long moment. "Tell me. Why do you care so much for Libby?"

"Why do you ask?"

"I probably should have asked this from the start, but I'm asking now. Out with it. What attracts you to her?"

"Really? You don't see it? She's got Proverbs 31 written all over her heart."

"And outside."

Evan blinked. "Gideon, she's the most beautiful woman I've ever met. Her almond-shaped green eyes, I've never seen eyes shine the way hers do. Her oval face. Her perfect lips." He stood. "I can't believe you have me talking like this. Turn the Three Stooges back on and see if I can laugh. It'll let me know if I've lost my manliness."

Gideon turned on the television but muted the sound.

Neither man smiled at the antics on the screen.

Gideon tossed down the remote. "Some idiots in this world don't see her outward beauty."

"Yeah, that jerk you set her up with, for one." Evan clenched his fist. "Wait—you're telling me you don't see it either?"

"Libby and my wife are like twins to me. God gave me Charisse. What I suspect is, unlike all the idiots in the world, you saw Libby's outer beauty before you ever knew what lay on the inside."

Evan nodded. "How could I not see it? I watched her with Charisse at Java Lava. I've seen her take a beating from my old man. I've watched Hope knock the wind out of her with her words, but Libby keeps on shining."

"So why haven't you stood up, beaten your chest, and claimed her—like a real man?"

Evan shook his head. "That's the old me. I've told you before. I don't want to hurt her, which is exactly what I do every time I get close to her."

Gideon leaned forward. "Do you think I would have ever gotten involved in Charisse's foolish plan to bring you two lovesick people together if I thought you'd hurt my wife's spiritual twin?"

"I understand that now, but before—this is new to me. I've always been selfish when it comes to relationships with the opposite sex. And here I am head over heels with Libby, and my previous relationships are steeped in parties and alcohol. And one of the women I know better than I should—she's with the woman I love. The ultimate irony."

Gideon smiled.

"What?" Evan shook his head.

"There's the proof I needed to give you permission to marry her."

"To marry her?"

"Yes, to marry her."

"What proof?"

"All these weeks of turmoil and upset have been caused by one thing." Gideon leaned forward. He pointed at Evan. "You've been trying to do what's best for Libby, even if it caused both of you pain. Evan, you've treated her with the utmost respect, resulting in nothing but misunderstanding between the two of you."

"Well?"

"Well, what?" Gideon looked to the television. The Three Stooges continued to batter each other.

"Do I have your blessing to marry Libby?"

"Yeah, if you can get her to say yes, after all the stupid things you've done." Gideon stretched.

Evan took a playful swing at Gideon's head. "That *I've* done? Don't go there after all the trouble you and Charisse have caused."

Gideon ducked, arms raised to protect himself. "Are you kidding? When the truth comes out, Ev, I'm taking full credit."

Evan narrowed his eyes and studied his friend. "What have you done?"

"You'll learn soon enough." Gideon laughed.

Evan sprang to his feet and started for the door.

Gideon beat him there and blocked his way. "Where do you think you're going?"

"To see Libby."

"Not on your life. You and me, Three Stooges marathon."

"What? Hope—"

"If Hope hasn't completely ruined it for you by now, she's not going to get the chance with Charisse and

Delilah there." Gideon turned him back toward the family room. "And I saw what my wife took over there to wear. They aren't expecting any men to show. Sit. Enjoy. Talk to her tomorrow."

"I'll go on home then."

Gideon eyed him. "Really? You have that much self-control? Uh-uh. Sit down. Prop your feet up. Enjoy the show. You can leave here in time to get ready for church, but otherwise, by the authority given to this judge of the Ninth Circuit Court in and for Orange County, Florida, bub, you're under house arrest."

Libby didn't care what she looked like. She wouldn't hurt the feelings of her new sister in Christ. When Hope turned her around to look into the mirror, she'd act as if Hope worked wonders.

Hope sniffled her way through the rest of the haircut and blow dry. She turned off the dryer and continued to fuss with Libby's hair. Standing away from Libby, she narrowed her gaze then she smiled. "Close your eyes."

Libby obeyed and tensed momentarily when Hope told her to stand, gripped her shoulders, and turned her to face the mirror. "Liberty Overstreet, meet the new and improved outer you."

Libby stared at the woman in the mirror then pivoted back to look at Hope.

Hope made her look back around. "So?"

"Is that really me?"

"That's you." Hope smiled. "Do you like?"

"I don't know what to say."

Delilah and Charisse pounded on the door. "Let us see. We've been waiting an hour," Charisse called.

"Hope, how did you do this?"

"Silly, I'm an artist. I see beauty in things I begin to love."

"So your friend who owns the salon, you made that up? You're the salon owner?"

Hope shook her head. "Libby, no. Like I said, I'm an artist. I paint. Evan didn't tell you?" Hope shook her head. "No, he didn't." She puffed out her cheeks and then released the air slowly. "That man. I don't know how he ever thought he could harm a woman. He's the most patient, loving, caring individual I've ever known—well, besides you."

Libby stared into the sink. And now Hope, a child of God, could love Evan in the way God intended.

"Hey." Hope made her turn. "What's wrong? The question you asked me earlier—you didn't really think we'd gotten into an argument, and he'd hurt me?"

Libby stared into Hope's blue eyes. "I have to admit that with what you told me I did doubt him for a second, but deep down, I knew Evan would never do that."

"But at Java. Libby, I saw his face. He was hurt that you thought he could have hurt me."

Libby blinked and shook her head. He'd been angry when he misunderstood her questioning, but he'd handled it well. "I really thought he'd been in the accident with you. It never occurred to me that he would hurt you, not until you were talking to me tonight."

"Then why did you tell him you thought he hated you?"

Libby coughed. "What?"

"Hey, come on out." Delilah banged on the door.

"Give it a rest, Dee. One more minute," Hope said and then turned her attention back to Libby. "Evan is under the impression you believe he hates you."

Libby tried to remember the conversation, regretting the careless words she'd flung at him.

"You said he hated you," Hope pressed. "Before you left us at Java."

Libby leaned her head back and stared up at the ceiling. "My dad." She leveled her gaze back to Hope. "I was talking about my dad. I need to call Evan and apologize. He's such a wonderful man." She looked at her image in the mirror. Pink flushed her cheeks. "But you know that."

"Yes, I do." Hope hugged her. "And we'll be sure to tell him that's not what you meant, but tonight is girls' night. Are you ready?" She held to the doorknob.

Libby nodded, and Hope opened the door.

Delilah stood with her mouth wide open.

Charisse laughed and reached for Libby. "Now everyone will see what I've seen in you all my life. Your inner and outer beauty."

Chapter Nineteen

Evan yawned and leaned against the counter by the coffeepot in the church's fellowship hall.

Gideon turned and kissed his wife as she greeted him.

"V.J.'s already in his Sunday school class. Did you get any sleep?" Gideon asked.

"I'm supposed to ask you that, I believe," she teased.

"He was asleep by ten o'clock," Evan muttered.

"And how would you know?" Charisse turned to him with a smile.

"I was shanghaied. V.J. was asleep before I arrived, and Gideon forced me to stay."

"Okay?" Charisse raised her brows. "Do I detect a little bit of disgruntlement?"

"A little?" Gideon laughed. "He wanted to run over there and crash your little slumber party. I had to make him stay."

"Well, come with me. I have a big surprise that might make you feel a hundred times better." Charisse linked her arm in Evan's and pulled him into the sanctuary.

Had Delilah and Charisse talked Libby into attending their church today and not driving to Titusville where she attended services?

"She has some news for you." Charisse pointed.

Hope stood beside Delilah.

Evan's shoulders fell. He didn't want to see Hope. He wanted to see Libby's beautiful face and keep his promise to Scarlet Trevetti.

"Don't look so glum. We're meeting Libby at her favorite restaurant after the service—all of us." Charisse pushed him forward.

"V.J.'s been asked to go to the park for a picnic with Bobby and his family." Gideon stood beside her. "We'll have to check and see if they won't mind watching him a little longer."

Charisse nodded to her husband and again pushed Evan toward Hope. "You'll want to talk to her. I promise."

Delilah moved away as Evan approached.

"Hope, I'm glad to see you here." Did his words ring true?

She turned toward him, a smile on her face.

For a girl who thought everything of beauty, she was brave to show up with the shaved spot on her head where the gash had been sewn.

"Evan," she breathed. "I did it. Libby showed me what all of you have. I prayed, and I have the hope you were talking about. I know I'll see Tiffany again one day."

Evan whooped, and everyone around him turned to look. He threw his arms around Hope. "That's great news. I'm so happy."

She pulled from his embrace and seemed to study him.

"What?" he asked.

"Libby was surprised to find out I'm an artist. You never told her you bought the painting, did you?" She put her hands on her slender hips.

He shook his head. "She loved it so much. I didn't want to disappoint her if you never gave it to me."

"Evan, I'm bad, but I'm not a thief. I would have given it to you eventually. Honestly, I wasn't holding on to it to torment Libby." She made a face. "Let me rephrase that so that I don't have to repent. Tormenting *you* wasn't the only reason I held on to it."

"Why then?"

"The little girl in the picture is me. The woman is my grandmother."

"Huh." Evan chuckled. "Libby said the artist took a page out of her life to draw it."

"I'd start to give it to you, but each time, I couldn't let it go."

"I understand. Look, if you want to paint Libby something else, I'll understand."

"No, the original belongs to her. I had a print done for me. I'm going to give you your money back, too."

He shook his head. "Keep it. You had that painting undervalued. In Libby's eyes it was priceless, and when she learns it's a portrait of you and your grandmother, it will be even more valuable." He hugged her again.

"She doesn't think you hate her, Evan, and at Java, it never entered her mind you'd done this to me. She was worried you'd been injured in an accident with me. She loves you so much."

Evan rubbed his tired eyes. He'd misread Libby and most likely hurt her once again with his accusations.

"Did you hear me? She loves you."

In what universe would he ever believe Hope would share this information with him? He smiled and pushed Hope's hair from her shoulder. "Thank you, Hope. I'm glad you were there for her. It might have scared me to death, but it means a lot to me."

She slipped her arm in his. "I became a new person last night. I'll try never to scare you again, old friend."

Evan parked his truck in the back lot of Titusville's nationally renowned restaurant, Dixie Crossroads, and walked toward the sprawling wooden building. Outside, he pushed his way through the crowd of people standing about the deck overlooking the fishpond. Kids leaned over the railing and threw pellets of fish food into the water.

"Hey." Gideon clamped his strong hand down on Evan's shoulder. "You could have ridden with us."

"I needed time to think," he said.

"Well, while you were thinking, we couldn't get a table because our entire party hadn't arrived. Thank you, Mr. Carter."

"What? Afraid your portly middle will shrink?" Delilah joined them.

"Excuse me?" Gideon released his breath and sucked in his stomach. "I'm still the fine-tuned athlete I was in high school."

"I think Charisse's cooking has you a little out of harmony." Delilah spun on her high heels and entered the restaurant's lobby.

"Hi," a shy voice lilted in Evan's direction.

How long had he waited to see her? Only a day, but it seemed an eternity. He started to turn, but Gideon's wide-eyed gaze stopped him. Then Gid let loose a whistle. "Wow."

"Get your tongue back into your mouth, Gideon Tabor," Charisse came beside her husband.

Evan looked in the direction of Gideon's opened-mouth stare.

Evan blinked. Her hair, a deep mahogany blend of colors highlighted her beautiful green eyes. A hint of makeup or a blush colored her cheeks a soft pink. "Wow," he repeated Gideon's declaration. "Libby, you've always been beautiful, but wow."

She lowered her eyes and stared at her feet. "Evan, I didn't know you were coming."

"Charisse told me we were all meeting here. I thought I was invited." He shifted. "I'm sorry. I didn't mean to crash the party." He swallowed down his disappointment.

A sad smile pushed its way onto her face. "Seems I'm always saying things to make you believe the opposite of what I mean." She touched his arm. "Evan, when we were at Java Lava yesterday, I didn't mean to imply you hated me. I was talking about someone else. I know you don't hate me, and I'm glad you can be here with Hope. This is a wonderful time to be together now that the Lord has made it possible for you—"

"They said they have our table if we can round everyone up." Delilah motioned from the door. "Come on. I'm hungry for some rock shrimp."

"Better do as she says, I know what's she's like when she's hungry." Gideon stepped ahead of them.

Evan held the door open for Libby. "I'm glad to be here with you, too." He told her as she passed.

Libby straightened her skirt and pressed her lips together.

"Libby, if you don't want me to bother you, all you have to do is say so."

Her green eyes filled with tears.

He put his hand on her shoulder. "Tell me what I've done this time. Let's work it out here and now. I don't ever want to hurt you again."

Libby shook her head, and the tears fell. "Excuse me." She pushed by him, spoke to Charisse, and the two of them hurried toward the restroom.

"What'd you do now?" Gideon stared at him.

"This way." The hostess started off, clearly expecting the party to follow.

"If I only knew." Evan leaned his head back to relieve the tension as he followed the hostess to the table, slipping his arm around Hope's shoulder as they walked.

Hope sent a sharp elbow into his side.

"Ouch." He pulled away. "And now I've done something to you, too. I'm beginning to believe I don't have a clue about women. You're beating me up. Libby doesn't want me here. What am I doing wrong?"

"Think!" Hope thumped him in the head with a finger. "You're trying to win the heart of one woman, and you slip your arm around another. And just so you know," Hope looked around him, "more than anyone else here, Evan, Libby wants you."

"She told you that?" Evan whispered.

"No, our prim and proper Libby would never voice something like that, but you better get it right this time. You're running out of chances with her."

Libby stared at her reflection in the mirror and at the likeness of Charisse who stood behind her. "I always thought that when you loved someone it would be a magical time. Despite what Mom went through, I thought I'd be deliriously happy."

Charisse fussed with Libby's hair. "See, that's the mistake most people make. Love isn't something you fall into. Love is a state of being. It's a lot like happiness. You love despite the troubles that come your way."

"That's the problem." Libby closed her eyes. "Despite everything I still love him. I've never been jealous of anything or anyone in my life, but Charisse, given the opportunity, I'd steal that man away from Hope in a heartbeat."

Charisse laughed. "I think you've already done that,

Libby. You just haven't opened yourself up to that possibility. That man is smitten with you."

"No. He's in love with Hope." Libby brushed the last remaining tears from her eyes. "And I have to love him enough to let them explore this new relationship, this one with Christ at their center."

Charisse's face lost all sense of humor. A frown replaced her smile. "Come on, Ms. Martyr. Let's go. If you're going to release him that easily, you deserve to have a front row seat." She stomped out of the restroom, the door falling closed behind her.

Libby took a deep breath and followed her friend. What did Charisse want her to do? Drag Evan out by his feet? Tell him he had to love her?

As she approached the table where everyone was already seated, Hope leaned across an empty chair and whispered to Evan.

Poor Evan. He'd made his decision. He loved Hope, but Libby's emotions probably plied him with guilt. Why else would he put a chair between himself and Hope except to spare Libby's feelings.

Libby made her way around the table to take her seat. "Hope, you need to sit here," she motioned, "by Evan."

Hope's eyes twinkled. "Libby, Evan saved that seat for you. He wouldn't let me sit in it if I wanted to." She made no move to change places.

Libby placed a smile on her face. "That isn't necessary, Evan. Let Hope sit by you." She wouldn't continue to confuse him.

"Sit down, Libby, please." Evan shook his head as if

her offer perplexed him.

Libby took a deep breath. *I can't do this, Lord. He's always been an all-or-nothing prayer for me. Please help me make it through this meal and show me how to stay out of his way.* She plopped into the seat.

The waitress brought the restaurant's signature corn fritters covered with confectionary sugar, and then she took their drink orders. When she left, Evan leaned toward Libby. "Would you come with me for one second?"

Libby shook her head. If the man had a problem understanding her emotions now, wait until he laid out his relationship with Hope, and Libby completely fell apart in front of him. "I can't do that right now. Please, wait and talk to me after we eat." Then she could run across the street to the cemetery and cry on my mother's headstone.

"No, I'm sorry. I can't wait. I'm beginning to believe my waiting for you has been our whole problem. If I have to spell it out in front of everyone, I guess that's what I have to do."

Libby gasped. Now she'd done it. He was going to end their friendship here in front of everyone. He'd given her a chance. Now, she'd have to live with her decision.

Evan toyed with his napkin, not looking at her. "I visited the nursing home yesterday afternoon, and I have a praise report, too. I met a woman named Scarlet."

"Scarlet Trevetti?" Libby didn't expect the conversation to take this turn, but she relaxed a bit. Maybe he wasn't going to destroy her now after all. Had

Scarlet talked to him like she said she wanted to do?

"Yeah." He tilted his head in her direction. "She had me going for a while. She told me her name was Scarlet Katie O'Hara."

The group erupted in laughter, and Libby covered her mouth with her napkin. That was Scarlet, all right.

"Turns out, I knew Scarlet when I was a kid." He shared a knowing look with Libby. "And Hope isn't the only one who came to know a loving Savior last night."

"That's great." Libby clasped her hands together. She'd sown some seeds there, but Evan saw the fruit. "I guess that means she talked to you about … other things."

"Yes, she did. She gave me a fine bit of wisdom." Evan's gaze bore into her. "And that's another praise report I have for you. See, the Lord used Scarlet to show me He had already answered one of my prayers. I've been praying for someone to love, but I've been afraid to accept the truth: I am capable of loving a woman without eventually harming her."

"So, you've fallen in love with Scarlet, a May-December romance?" Gideon laughed.

Libby gave Gideon a pointed stare, and he backed down like a scolded puppy. Well, at least his meddling had resulted in something good.

"Scarlet helped me put a lot of things in perspective," Evan continued.

Here it came. He was about to lower the boom. Sure, he sneaked some good news in to lessen the blow, but it didn't help. She steeled herself for the truth.

"She showed me something I never stopped to

consider. Sometimes the evil a person is forced to live with makes them stronger rather than weaker. I always thought of myself as a victim of Nate's violence. Instead I've triumphed over the demons in Nate's life that caused him to treat my family the way he did." His brown eyes settled once again on Libby.

Libby scooted her chair back a bit so Evan could see around her to the woman he loved.

His intense stare never left Libby's face. "I know now without a doubt I'd never harm someone who loves me. I would do the exact opposite." He placed his hand on the back of Libby's chair. "I would protect her from those who would cause her harm. I did it with my mother. I protected her from Nate. For you, I protected you twice, once with Nate and the other with that jerk Gideon set up." He took a deep breath and let it out. "This is harder than I thought, Libby."

He didn't know the half of it.

Evan placed his hand over hers. Libby sent an apologetic look in Hope's direction, but when Evan gave her hand a soft squeeze, she looked back to him. "I might have been wrong in what I did, but my actions were meant to protect you," he said.

"I knew that." She never doubted his reasons. But why was he telling her all this—to keep her heart from breaking? Too late.

"Libby, I'd never intentionally hurt you. I thought I might be able to. I kept trying to protect you from my world, never realizing the Lord had answered my prayer.

Despite loving you with all my heart, I feared letting you in because I thought I'd harm you, take away your innocence, and you'd eventually lose the sweetness that attracted me to you from the start, your nature that wouldn't allow me to let you go."

Libby pulled her hand away from his and brought it down hard on the table. "You can't do this. You can't tell Hope you love her and then tug at my heart like this."

Hope's laughter boomed through the restaurant. All motion around them stopped. "Libby, Evan never said he loved me. What made you think …?"

Libby turned on Evan. He couldn't play with her heart—with Hope's heart—this way. "At Tiffany's funeral. You said you loved Hope."

Evan leaned back, his eyes wide. "That's why you left us so quickly that day? Libby, I might be guilty of taking my time to understand what God has for us, but from the very first day we were introduced, you've run away when things hurt you. Baby, if you'd stayed and talked to me, even at the gardens when I left you to talk to Hope …" His gaze left Libby, staring behind her.

Libby turned, and Hope stopped shaking her head.

Evan touched Libby's chin with his finger, drawing her back to him. "I went back to talk to Hope, but it had everything to do with my love for you and not her. She knows this. We've talked it out. Hope knows despite our past together—something I'll fully explain to you—Libby Overstreet, I love you." He reclaimed her hand. "At the funeral, we got our signals crossed. You were talking about Hope. I was thinking about Tiffany. I did love

Tiffany. She was my friend, and she's gone."

"The boy loved you even before Hope made you into this gorgeous woman we see today," Delilah quipped.

Evan pointed his finger at Delilah. "She's always been beautiful, Dee. Always."

He thinks I'm beautiful.

He—he loves me.

"Oh, Libby, you once gave me this same advice." Charisse clasped her hands together in a plea. "Please listen to this man."

Libby's lips trembled. "You love me?" she whispered to Evan.

"I have loved you since the moment I laid eyes on you in Java Lava. You looked up at me, and you pressed your sweet little lips together. Your green eyes widened behind those wonderfully overlarge glasses, and I was intrigued at what you saw in me that made your cheeks turn crimson."

He loved her. This couldn't be happening. What would come next to shatter the illusion?

"I love you so much that it'll take a lifetime for me to show you." Evan squeezed her hand again.

"Do you intend to start showing her this afternoon?" Charisse bounced up and down in her seat like a small child.

Libby looked from Evan to Charisse and back to Evan.

"If she'll let me." He brushed her hair back over her shoulder. "Will you let me?"

"Oh, yes." Libby pressed her hand against her chest. She couldn't see his face clearly through the tears pooling in her eyes, but she felt his lips brush gently against hers. Then, he kissed her harder, his embrace tightening around her.

All those weeks ago, she'd been wrong. His touch had been ecstasy, but his kiss was heavenly.

"Evan," she whispered. "I love you, too." She bit her lip for a moment. Her stubbornness had made this very private man declare his love for her in front of their friends.

"Libby?" He waited. "Is something wrong?"

"No, but since you've been so open with everyone, maybe I should tell you the truth."

He cleared his throat and looked down. "What?"

She placed her hand against his cheek until he looked at her. "When I saw you that first time in Java Lava, those thoughts that turned my face red—I wondered what it would be like to feel your kiss on my lips."

Gideon and Charisse high-fived, and the group broke into cheers. "They're in love." Gideon stood and pointed down to Libby and Evan. "And I'm the man who convinced them."

The restaurant cheered.

Gideon sat. "I'm glad that's over. These two have made life miserable for Charisse and me. And to think, a little old lady named Scarlet Renee Trevetti did what I couldn't do after all these weeks of trying." He winked at Evan.

Evan narrowed his eyes. "How do you know her

middle name?" He turned his gaze toward Libby, his forehead still touching hers.

"Just a lucky guess." Gideon laughed. "Or maybe the one step ahead you thought you had on me was actually about twenty behind."

Evan ignored his friend and kissed Libby once again. "I don't want to risk one more disaster. Please say you'll marry me?"

"It's okay, Lib. I gave the man permission to ask. After all, I'm the one responsible for you." Gideon stuck out his chest, reminding her of a proud peacock.

"Not for long, Gideon." Libby smiled at her fiancé. "Not for too much longer, I pray."

Chapter Twenty

Libby sat nervously on the edge of Charisse and Gideon's couch. Evan sat beside her, his head bowed.

"We'll be in the kitchen until you call us." Gideon followed Charisse out of the room.

"Evan," Libby whispered his name. "You know this isn't necessary."

"Yes, Libby, it is," he said, but he didn't move.

She waited, her heart breaking for him. "I love you. This doesn't matter."

Evan's brown eyes looked into her soul. "I know I'm better than Nate is …" His words trailed, and his jaw lifted with the clench of his teeth. Evan was trying hard to keep a hold of his emotions. "That's not true."

"Evan—"

"No." He stopped her with the quietly spoken word. "I'm not better than Nate." With a warm hand, he reached to touch Libby's hair. "I'm a man, and I have my imperfections, but because of Nate's flaws, I know what it's like to see the people you love hurt by your actions. Nate hurt me in ways I'll never hurt you."

"Don't you think I know this?" Libby reached and held her hand in his. "I trust you, Evan. We don't have to go through this."

"But it's deeper than that, Libby." His brown eyes

filled with so much pain, Libby could barely stand to look into their depths. "You have to know what you get when you get me. There isn't any turning back after we marry. I won't let you go. I've worked too hard to get you."

They both shared a simple laugh.

"Libby, I didn't care what others thought, because they didn't mean what you mean to me."

"Nothing could make me leave. You must know that." Even his declaration that there had been others before her.

Evan stood, and Libby's heart raced. Her experience with men was so sheltered that the intimacy was hard for her.

He unbuttoned his shirt and slipped it off his shoulders.

Libby's face felt afire as he stared down at her, his broad muscles and tan skin taking her breath away and making her tremble with desire.

"I'm sorry," Evan whispered as he turned his back to her.

Libby fought the gasp. For several seconds, she couldn't speak.

Evan stood, his head lowered. His shoulders began to shake, and she realized that he was sobbing.

Libby stood. She reached out and touched the scars.

Evan jumped when her fingertips lighted on the scarred tissue, but he didn't look up. His entire body went rigid.

"How did he do it?" She deliberately made her words strong.

Evan took a deep breath. "He took a steel bar and put it into the flames of our grill. Then he laid it on my back until it seared my skin."

Libby ran her hand along each of the six different scars. Six times, Nate had burned his son. Six times, Evan had felt his flesh burn. She couldn't imagine the agony.

"Why did he do it?"

Evan started to lift his shirt on, but Libby stopped him with a tug.

He turned to her.

"Why did he do it, Evan?"

When he finally looked her in the face again, the tears spilled. "Because I was a coward. I hid in a closet while he beat my mother. I never hid again."

Libby moved around him once again and, if possible, Evan's body tensed even more than it had before. This time she moved closer to him.

She'd never done anything so bold before, but he needed to know the truth. She pressed her lips against his scar.

He turned and enfolded her in his arms. "God has been so good to me. So good to bring you into my life. I will never let anyone harm you. I'll never hurt you, not like Nate did to my mother, my brothers, and me."

Libby clung to him. "I never thought you would." If he'd only kiss her again like he did in the restaurant.

Her body tingled in a way that she wasn't used to. She stepped away from him. "Evan, I can't think clearly. I think we need to—"

As if sensing her desire, he smiled at her. "Me, too, Libby. Me, too. Why do you think I insisted on doing this here with the two goofs in the other room?"

"That would be Mr. and Mrs. Matchmaker Supreme Goofs to you." Gideon came around the corner followed by his wife. "And put your shirt on. My wife doesn't need to see what manual labor does to a body. She'll want me out there carrying wood and hammering nails right alongside you."

Evan's nerves calmed as Libby slipped her warm hand into his. He smiled at her when they reached Nate's room. In her other hand, Libby carried a Bible. *Thank you, Father, for this one beside me. I'm not wasting any time. I pray she'll understand why I can't wait to make this wise one my Proverbs 31 woman.*

Once God cleared the way, Evan had determined not to squander another moment. Gideon and Charisse had all but carried them to the Clerk of Court the Monday following his proposal. There, they'd waited while Evan and Libby filed for their license to marry.

Evan knocked on the door. He shared a look of surprise with Libby when Nate's stern voice bid them entry. Not for lack of trying, but Libby had not visited Nate since the night he nearly killed her. Now, she stood behind Evan, almost pressing into his back. She might be afraid of his father, but she wasn't afraid of him.

"My little angel," Nate addressed her. "I wondered

where you'd gone."

"Mr. Carter, it's so good to see you again." Libby moved next to Evan but did not approach his father.

Nate's gaze moved to the Bible in Libby's hand. He stared at it for a long moment, and Evan tensed. The squeeze of Libby's hand in his took away his own fear.

"Mr. Carter, we brought something for you." Libby held out the Bible they'd bought together.

Nate hesitated for a moment then took it.

"Evan and I have been praying for you."

Nate blinked but did not look up from the leather-bound book with his name engraved in gold on the cover.

Evan swallowed, "I know you probably don't care about this, but I wanted to let you know I've forgiven you."

Nate squirmed.

"For everything, *Dad*."

Nate's hand trembled in its hold on the Bible. "You say you have, but saying and doing are two different things."

"I might have to do it three or four times a day, but I turn it over to God. I leave you in God's hands, but I choose to love you."

"Thanks." Nate's tone resonated with sarcasm and brought a twinge of a smile to Libby's lips.

"Mr. Carter, Evan wanted to give you some important news."

Nate waited in silence while Evan formed the words. "I love Libby, and I've asked her to marry me."

When Nate looked at Libby and smiled, Evan wondered where the anger had gone.

"Thank you," Nate whispered. The Bible slipped from his hand.

Libby caught it before it fell to the ground.

Nate reached, and Libby placed it in his grasp again, holding her hand to his. Nate closed his eyes tight and then opened them. "Thank you for loving my son. I never showed him any of it. I don't know where he got it from. He's always been different than me—better than me."

"Mr. Carter, I don't understand why you treated your family badly, but God knows all about you."

"I'm afraid he does." Nate swallowed hard.

"Well, the good news is He cares for you." Libby sat on the bed beside Evan's father.

Evan moved close in case Nate's mood changed.

Libby smiled up at Evan and then returned her attention to his father. "God cares why you did the things you did, and He cares about what happened to you to cause the pain to erupt the way it did."

"I'm sure He kept score."

"Yeah, He has," Evan interjected. "But he'll erase the score if you ask Him to do it."

"How will He do that?"

Without hesitation, Libby took the Bible from Nate's hand and opened it to the Scriptures that God had given them. Evan breathed a prayer of thanks for Nate's calm lucidity and prayed for the Holy Spirit to speak to the man who'd terrorized him most of his life. He prayed so hard he lost track of the discussion between Libby and his father until he heard Nate say, "Amen." Then, he looked into the tear-stained face of his future bride.

"Mr. Carter, when Evan and I are married, may I call you Dad, too?"

Nate nodded and turned to look out the window. "I'm not always here, you know."

"But God knows where to find you, Dad," Evan whispered. "Even when we can't."

Libby graced his father with a tenuous kiss on his cheek.

Nate turned wide eyes to her. He touched his face where Libby had shown him her loving tenderness. "Thank you."

"Good night." Evan reached for Libby's hand. "We'll be back soon." He led Libby out of the room.

In the hallway, Evan caught sight of a dressed-to-the-nines Scarlet Trevetti. The older woman couldn't roll her wheelchair out of sight quick enough, even with Charisse and Gideon behind her. In his haste to push Scarlet around the corner, Gideon slid on something on the floor. Charisse's giggle filled the air.

"Was that Charisse?" Libby started to turn toward the distraction.

Those three matchmakers had worked hard to bring Evan and Libby together, but they would blow his surprise if he didn't think fast. Evan fought his own laughter and pulled Libby into his embrace. "I love you, you know."

"Oh, yes, I know." She peered up at him. "I'll never

doubt that again. I promise."

It'd been all he could do not to kiss her since their first two kisses at the restaurant two weeks before. He'd been reckless with his relationships in the past. Libby's love was a precious gift, and he wanted to wait for the proper moment. Now, with the longing in her eyes he had to fight the strong urge to cover her mouth with his. "Let's go get ready for our date." He slipped his arm over her shoulder and led her to his truck.

Libby reached across the seat and laced her fingers with Evan's outstretched hand. He turned his truck onto the highway and took the next exit. He'd asked her to dress up for the evening, mentioning dinner at 310 Lakeside, the restaurant where their first misunderstanding had taken place, but he'd just taken a wrong turn.

"Evan, 310 Lakeside is in the other direction?"

"I know." An irresistible smile turned his lips.

She narrowed her eyes. "Where are you taking me?"

"Trust me." He squeezed her hand.

She sat back. He would be her husband soon. She needed to have faith in him. If she'd trusted him from the beginning, there would have been less pain for both of them. After all, she was dressed up fancy. Wherever they were going would be special. Evan didn't look too shabby in his black suit and red tie either.

He pulled into the parking lot of the storefront where the church he attended with Charisse, Gideon, and Delilah assembled. She waited as Evan exited the truck, came around to her side, opened the door, and helped her down.

"Now, will you tell me what's going on?" she asked.

"Only after you answer a question for me."

"One question?"

"One very important question." He bent down on one knee and gazed up at her.

"Oh." A rush of heat warmed her cheeks. "Evan, you'll ruin your suit."

"Libby Overstreet, will you, right this minute, without hesitation, marry me?"

His brown eyes held so much anticipation, as if he thought she'd run away. Where would he have gotten that idea? Despite his seriousness, she couldn't help but smile. "Evan. I already said yes."

"No, baby. Listen to the question carefully."

She loved it when he called her *baby.* She'd never get tired of hearing it, and now, the sound of it took her focus away.

He bowed his head for a second and then looked back to her. "Libby Overstreet, will you, right this minute, without hesitation, marry me?"

The significance of his words held her silent. She began to tremble with anticipation. He wanted her to marry him, to make her his wife, to never be separated from this day forward. "Right now? This very minute?"

"Right now, this minute?" he repeated. His gaze went

to the heavens. "Dear God, let her say yes."

"Dear God, how could I ever say no when You've given me the desire of my heart, and he wants to be my husband." Libby stared up into the early evening stars and then looked down at her prince. "Yes, Evan, yes. This very minute. Please." She pulled him from his knees and wrapped her arms around his waist.

The doors of the building opened, and a group of people flooded out.

Gideon Tabor stepped between them. "None of this until it's official."

Charisse rushed forward, wearing a beautiful long black dress. She reached out her hand toward Libby and pulled her inside the church. Charisse headed into a room to the left of the sanctuary, but Libby stopped her. Red roses adorned the main auditorium.

"You wanted a black and white wedding, right?" Charisse asked. "That dream hasn't changed?"

"Charisse, did you do all this?"

"We all worked on it." Charisse hugged her. "Gideon wants to give you away if that's all right with you?"

"I bet he can't wait." Libby laughed.

"You're also going on your dream honeymoon." Charisse beamed. "Tahiti will never be the same once Libby Overstreet Carter comes for a visit."

Libby gasped. "You can't do that."

Charisse ignored her. "As your self-appointed matron of honor, my husband and I can do whatever we want to be a blessing to you. Don't you know you're like a sister to me? Besides V.J. doesn't need his college fund for another ten years." She winked.

Libby hugged her again and looked once more into the decorated room. Scarlet Trevetti rolled into sight. Libby smiled and waved.

"Evan wouldn't hear of her not joining you for this day. He arranged it with the nursing home. We discussed bringing his father, but Evan thought he was too volatile, and he wants this evening to be wonderful for you." Charisse wiped a tear from her eyes. "That man of yours really is someone special, Libby."

Libby nodded. "He's my answer to prayer. Of course he's special."

Charisse laughed. "Hope and Delilah wanted to give us a minute, but they've agreed to be your bridesmaids." She led Libby into a side room.

"Let them try to get out of it."

"And I'd like for you to wear this." Charisse moved toward a closet inside the room and pulled out a beautiful white wedding gown.

"This isn't the dress you wore when you married Gideon," Libby noted.

"No, this is my gown from my wedding with Vance. Of course, I've taken it in quite a few inches. We both know I was a lot bigger back then. I've been working on it since Gideon and I first started trying to get the two of you together."

Libby touched the dress. "I'd wear it whether it fit or not."

"Now, do you forgive Gideon and me for our

meddling?"

"Since it turned out so well, I guess I can't hold a grudge." Libby continued to run her fingers over the beautiful lace of the gown. "But why did you work so hard? You should have given up when I let go of my dreams."

"Because the first time I saw Evan look in your direction, I was floored with the love on his face. I'd never seen a man drink in a woman the way he did you." She brushed Libby's hair. "And when I turned to look at the person he was staring at, I saw the same look in your pretty green eyes. I knew his history, and it worried me, but Gideon told me Evan had character. Then Gid took control of the operation. And you know his determination."

The door to the room opened, and Hope and Delilah rushed in. Both of them wore a similar style black dress as the one Charisse wore.

Libby giggled. "I suppose you went to the fitting for these even before you knew Evan and I would finally get this right?"

"Delilah and I did, but Hope's was a rush order." Charisse hugged Libby.

"If you don't get a move on, Evan is going to have a heart attack." Hope unzipped Libby's dress. "Let's see how this gown fits. We brought safety pins just in case."

"Safety pins won't work. I bought something that'll work better." Delilah held up a brightly colored stapler. "Something new and blue."

Libby waited at the edge of the doorway of the rose-filled sanctuary. Her eyes remained on the man standing to the side of the pastor. Evan lifted his gaze to her, and Libby smiled before turning her attention to the man at her side. "Thank you, Gideon." She squeezed his arm linked with hers.

"I told Evan I imagine you as Charisse's twin sister. Two beautiful women with the same Christ-filled heart. Libby, I love you, girl. There's nothing Charisse and I won't do for you and for that dope standing at the front of the church."

She peered up at him. "You didn't give up on us when we couldn't find our way to each other. I'm so glad you stayed in there pushing us together. The *dope* and I love you, too."

"Don't think for a minute that guy would ever give up on you. He might have stepped back a time or two, but Libby, he loves you as much as I love Charisse. That's the only reason I worked so hard to make this happen."

"May I ask? How did you get Scarlet involved?"

"My bailiff, Bill, is her son-in-law. She's an ex-deputy sheriff, and Bill told me they had to move her into the home because he and his wife both work different hours. I visited Nate every now and then because I knew Evan wasn't, and the guilt was weighing on him. I thought I'd check in on Scarlet, too." He shrugged as if his concern wasn't endearing him even more to Libby. "I

asked one of the nurse's there to introduce me to her, and
Scarlet is the ears and eyes of that nursing home. All the
nurses, aides, and the residents there love you, and they
knew how you felt about Evan. I think Scarlet likes to
gossip a bit. She told me about Evan's childhood, and
how she knew him, and said what a shame it was that you
two were struggling to get to know each other." He leaned
over. "And that's when Scarlet became my accomplice."

The music began, and she stepped down the aisle
with Gideon.

They came to a stop in front of the pastor.

Libby gave a nervous look to her intended. A shiver
of delight ran down her spine.

"Who gives this woman to this man?" the pastor
asked.

The warmth of Gideon's hand covering the fingers
that held to his strong forearm gained her attention.
Gideon winked. "With God's blessing, her sister and her
brother do." He kissed her cheek and stepped back
releasing her to her future.

Evan moved beside her. He lifted his open hand. In it,
he carried the red tatted cross she'd given him at their
accidental meeting at the nursing home.

How did she ever deserve this wonderfully
sentimental, godly man?

She placed her hand in his, both of their palms
wrapped around the cross. The pastor gave a few opening
remarks and then asked Evan to say his vows—ones he'd
obviously taken time to write and to memorize.
"Rollercoaster rides are fun, aren't they?" He smiled at

her. "They're harrowing and seemingly dangerous. Your heart falls to your feet and then the blood rushes to you head. You don't know if you're upside down or downside up. Then the ride comes to an end, and you wish you'd enjoyed the experience more and worried less."

Libby bit her lip and widened her eyes. The poor man. She'd put him through so much.

"Libby Overstreet, I wouldn't change a moment of our courtship because it allowed me to see inside the heart of the woman I love more than my own life. I came to realize that there is nothing I won't do to protect you. The ups and downs, the crazy turns—they all made me understand that you are to be honored, and I'm so glad God has given you to me to protect and to hold—to cherish."

Lord, you've answered my prayers—the ones I lifted to you from the very beginning.

"Libby," the pastor said, "Evan said he didn't tell you about his vows, and if you want, I could …"

Libby shook her head. She reached and grasped Evan's free hand in hers. "Evan Carter, I know that you are not only the result of my prayers lifted to our heavenly Father. You are the answer to my mother's prayers. She petitioned the Lord each night for a man who would love me and take care of me in her absence. God saw to it that I learned first that I could lean upon Him. The lesson was a hard one for me, but I know that everything we have been through only strengthened our love for one another. And I know the importance of having a husband I can trust with not only my heart, but in every aspect of my life." She looked down at their hands then looked him straight in the eyes. "I cherish you, Evan Carter. I place my life in your hands. I trust you, and I will honor you all the days of our lives."

She waited. Evan had not kissed her again since the kiss at the restaurant, and it was all she dreamed of these days.

"Libby, before I officially declare you husband and wife, Evan has asked for the opportunity to make a promise to you and to those gathered here to celebrate your marriage."

Evan's gorgeous smile reached his brown puppy dog eyes, and Libby realized that her groom probably had not rested in days. She felt the fabric of the cross they held.

"Baby, we've had a lot of misunderstandings along the rocky road that led us down this aisle. In front of our friends and our families," he nodded to those gathered close to them, to Gideon, Charisse, Delilah, and to Hope, "I want you to understand I do not take your love lightly. I will never raise my hand to you in anger. I accept with the greatest respect this responsibility God has given to me as your protector. And I am overwhelmed that God would give into my hands someone as wonderful and as beautiful as Liberty Overstreet to cherish and to honor. May today be the first of many happily-ever-afters."

"Oh, Evan ..." With a trembling hand, she wiped at her tears.

"Evan Carter, you may kiss your bride," the pastor said.

Evan leaned toward her. A sob broke forth from him as his lips touched hers. She held fast to him as his kiss swept her away.

When he leaned back from the kiss, he brushed her cheek with a tender hand. "I am thankful God has been so gracious to grant me Liberty to love."

Chapter Twenty-One

Again, Libby was in a vehicle with Evan driving in the opposite direction of their destination. She turned in the seat of her car—their car now. "Evan, the plane's going to leave without us. We're going the wrong way again. We'll never get through security in time."

"I lied to you, Mrs. Carter. The plane leaves two hours later than I said." He lifted the back of her hand to his lips.

"Evan." She pulled from his hold, feigning disbelief.

Last night when he'd taken off his shirt in their honeymoon suite, he'd been shy about allowing her to see the scars on his back again. The thought of what he'd been through and what had caused him to believe he could harm her had taken her breath away. In the darkness, as he'd held her in his arms, she had caressed what had brought him the shame. "Evan," she'd whispered, "Because of these … because you bear them and you still bear Nate's care, I know that the man I married is kind, loving, and forgiving. I will never mistrust you or your actions again."

And Evan had cried. "If we look to God for guidance, if we love Him and offer love and trust to each other, everything will fall into place."

He took her hand now, waking her from her

memories of the sweetest moments alone with him as husband and wife. "Trust me, baby?"

"You ask me to trust you, and you lie to me? I never!" She fanned herself like a true Southern Belle. "What are you up to, Mr. Carter?"

"You'll see."

Libby laced her fingers in his once again. They had been married exactly fourteen hours, and she still needed his touch to believe God's goodness toward her.

"Now, would you do me a favor?"

"I don't know. You lied to me."

"You won't regret it. Now, close your eyes and start counting down slowly from thirty."

"Not another surprise."

"When you finish counting down, I'll show you."

Libby did as he asked, slowly ticking down the numbers. She was still counting when the car stopped, and Evan turned off the engine.

"Ten ..."

Evan opened his own door. "Keep going, and keep your eyes shut."

"Nine ... eight ... seven ... six ..."

The door opened, and Evan guided her out. "Keep counting."

"Five ... four ..."

They walked a few feet.

"Three ... two ... one. Can I open them now?"

"Uh-huh."

She looked through narrowed eyes and then opened them wide. She placed her hand to her rapidly beating heart. "You didn't?" She could barely get the question out. "Evan, you didn't?"

"Well, what do you think?" He beamed.

Libby stepped forward. The garden nursery—her dream—he'd renovated it and landscaped the property around the business. Before her eyes, the renderings he'd drawn for her came to life. The cottage was painted and had a new roof. He'd added a front deck and a back deck. The store where she'd provide inventory of garden tools and a variety of other garden related items was rebuilt, the rusting metal building had been replaced by a large wooden structure to match the overall theme of the business. The greenhouse stood tall and proud with its new panes of glass installed. Meandering cobblestone paths led to patches of bare ground where she would place her inventory of trees, shrubs, and plants. "Evan," she breathed his name. "It's wonderful."

"I had it almost completed for you when I didn't think we had a chance. I know our circumstances have changed. You may not want the place now."

She twirled around like a girl of five, feeling the exhilaration of the moment. Then she stopped, remembering she wasn't alone any longer. She had a husband, and he would always be her first priority. "You won't mind if I do this?"

"Libby, look around and see if I mind."

"The cottage …"

"I initially planned it as a home for you, but it's an office now—our offices, actually. I nixed the plans to build the one at home. When I'm not at a worksite, I'll be underfoot. Think of the business we can both get from each venture. My clients might be looking for landscape ideas, and your clients might be looking for an architect or a contractor for anything from a gazebo to a mansion." He leaned back. "I think God knew what he was doing when he brought us to each other's attention, don't you think?"

"Oh, so it's not all about loving me." She laughed.

Evan didn't smile. "No, Libby. It *is* all about my love for you. If you told me you really didn't want the business, I'll be fine with it. Whatever makes you happy."

Libby touched her husband's face. "Our cottage office and this property will be a wonderful place for the kids to play while Daddy and Momma work."

His smile returned. "Whew, that was close."

She swatted at him.

He took her hand and led her to the cottage. "Will you close your eyes for me one more time?" He placed a key into the lock.

"Really?" She feigned aggravation. "I don't know. Each time you surprise me, I nearly faint. Your next surprise might be too exciting for me."

He tilted his head to the side. "This is the last time— at least for today. I promise." He brushed a kiss against her cheek. "But I do plan to surprise you as often as I can."

"Okay, if you insist," she teased and closed her eyes.

"So, how many kids are we going to have?" He placed his arm around her. "No peeking."

"As many as you can love." She held out her hand to keep from bumping into anything as he led her through the door.

"My love is boundless, Libby."

She swallowed down the emotion his words stirred in her heart. "Thank you for loving me."

"Not a problem." His low chuckle made her laugh. "Okay." With a tender hand, he raised her chin upward. "You can open them."

Libby blinked behind her glasses. "Oh, Evan." She stared up at the painting hanging above the marble mantel of a gorgeous and eye-catching fireplace. The portrait that captured her heart on their first date to the Harry P. Leu Garden art exhibit—the painting she'd never forgotten. The old woman's face stared down at the beautiful little girl.

She turned into his embrace. "I can't believe it. I've never been able to get this picture out of my mind. I miss my mother and grandmother so much, and this enhances my good memories of them."

"Look closer at the signature, and tell me if you can make it out."

She clung to him for a long moment before looking back at the painting. She studied the name and gasped. "Hope?"

"I went back to buy this for you. Of course, she made me work for it. Then she didn't get it to me as soon as she promised. When you misunderstood, I had no proof to show you why I went back. I decided not to say anything.

You were right all along."

"About what?" She leaned against him.

"Hope is the little girl. The woman is her grandmother."

"And she let you buy this. Evan, we can't do that. It's got to be precious for her."

Evan reached in his pocket and handed her a card. "She thought you might say that. Here's her answer."

Libby opened the card.

Libby, don't believe a word the guy says.

She looked at Evan. "Did you read this?"

He shook his head.

She looked back down at Hope's expressive penmanship.

If Evan tells you he loves you, please know the man loves you in a way few women have ever been loved. That boy would die for you. He almost did the day he asked to purchase my painting, and while he did not die, he did pay dearly for it—monetarily, and in the time it cost him away from you.

Evan says this painting reminded you of your grandmother. If your mother or your grandmother loved you as much as my Grams loved me, I know this portrait will continue to wrap their love around you each time you see it—the way you wrap your love around everyone you meet.

Thank you, Libby, for caring enough to show me the greatest love in all the world.

Your "new" friend and sister, Hope.

Evan slipped his arm around her, and as always, she

trembled at his touch. "I can't imagine what she had to say."

Libby kissed his cheek. "She told me I'm the luckiest woman in the entire world, Evan Carter."

He searched her face. "Libby Carter, happy endings don't happen by luck. They're God driven, and you, my Cinderella, are more than I ever dreamed could come true. Of course, I had to run after you to get you to try on the shoe, but the trouble was well worth it."

Holding to his hand, she twirled, falling back into his arms. "Well, Mr. Carter, this Cinderella will never scurry away from you again. Right now, she wants her handsome prince to take her on her Tahitian honeymoon. When we return, I'll work on opening up our new business, Happily-Ever-After Gardens."

Discussion Questions

1. Libby's full name is actually Liberty, as in the liberty that we have in Christ. Some mistake this liberty as the authorization to do whatever we want because we have that "free pass" to Heaven. In Christ, the liberty we have is to serve Him. Libby's name is important because of the liberty that she refuses to take in her relationship with Christ. Libby is a daughter of the King, but in so many ways, she refuses to believe this. Where do you see this failing in Libby's life? Do you see the same kind of failing in your life?

2. Libby's self-perception is a poor one. She can't believe that anyone like Evan would be interested in her. Evan, on the other hand, believes he can never be the man that Libby deserves. Where did the misconception in these two individuals develop? Do you have any similar thoughts about yourself? If so, take a minute to look at yourself through the eyes of a loving, Father who tells us that we are each wondrously made (Psalm 139:14), and write down at least five things that God loves about you.

3. Libby's character and her actions speak into the lives of others, and she doesn't seem to know it. Why do you suppose that is true and why do her actions have such an impact on those around her?

4. Hope's friend Tiffany died, but even in sadness her friends can rejoice. What about you? If you were to die today, could your friends be heartened by the fact that they will someday see you again? Have you taken the same steps that Tiffany (and Hope) did to assure that you not only have liberty to serve Christ here on this earth but that you also will have eternal life to serve Him in Heaven?

About the Author

Fay Lamb's emotionally charged stories remind the reader that God is always in the details. Fay has contracted with Write Integrity Press for three series. *Stalking Willow* and *Better than Revenge,* Books 1 and 2 in the Amazing Grace romantic suspense series are currently available for purchase. *Charisse* and *Libby,* the first two novels in her Ties That Bind contemporary romance series have been released. Fay has also collaborated on three romance  novellas: *The Christmas Tree Treasure Hunt, A Ruby Christmas,* and *A Dozen Apologies.* Her adventurous spirit has taken her into the realm of non-fiction with *The Art of Characterization: How to Use the Elements of Storytelling to Connect Readers to an Unforgettable Cast.*

Future Write Integrity Press releases from Fay are: *Everybody's Broken* and *Frozen Notes*, Books 3 and 4 of *Amazing Grace* and *Hope* and *Delilah*, Books 3 and 4 from The Ties that Bind. Also, look for Book 1 in Fay's Serenity Key series entitled *Storms in Serenity.*

Fay and her husband, Marc, reside in Titusville, Florida, where multi-generations of their families have lived. The legacy continues with their two married sons and six grandchildren.

Visit Fay on the Web:
www.FayLamb.com

More Books by Fay Lamb

Charisse
Book One in the
Ties that Bind Series

Charisse Wellman's husband has been gone a year, and she's about to lose the only home her son, V.J., has ever known. She's quit law school but the money just isn't there. Her only option is to work as a law clerk for her ex-friend, Gideon Tabor. The only problem: Gideon is the judge who let her husband's killer go free, and Gideon doesn't know the connection.

Gideon Tabor can't believe that the woman interviewing for the job is the girl he loved in high school. Charisse is hesitant about accepting his job offer, and when she does, Gideon makes every attempt to apologize for his relationship-ending blunder in high school. Charisse accepts his apology, but she keeps him at a distance. When Gideon learns that Charisse's anger actually stems from his release of the man who ran down her husband, he tries to explain, but Charisse doesn't want Gideon's excuses or the love he has to offer. She wants her husband's killer to pay.

Available on Amazon, Kindle, Barnes & Noble, and other booksellers by request.

Coming Soon:
Hope and *Delilah*

Stalking Willow
Book One in the Amazing Grace Series

Bitterness, a stalker, and a neighbor to die for. What's a girl to do? Trailed by a stalker in New York City, Willow Thomas, a young ad executive, scurries back to her small North Carolina hometown and the lake house where ten years earlier a scandal revealed her entire life had been a lie, and a seed of bitterness took root in her soul.

The cocoon of safety Willow feels upon her arrival home soon unravels when she meets opposition from her family, faces the man she left behind, and the stalker reveals he is close on her heels.

Can Willow learn to trust God to tear out her roots of resentment, reunite her family, ferret out a deadly stalker, and to rekindle the love she left behind?

Better Than Revenge
Book Two in the Amazing Grace Series

Michael's fiancée, Issie Putnam, was brutally attacked and Michael was imprisoned for a crime he didn't commit. Now he's home to set things right.

Two people stand in his way: Issie's son, Cole, and a madman.

Can Michael learn to love the child Issie holds so close to her heart and protect him from the man who took everything from Michael so long ago?

Available on Amazon, Kindle, Barnes & Noble, and by order from your favorite bookseller.

Coming Soon:

Look for other books

published by

Pix-N-Pens Publishing

www.PixNPens.com

and

www.WriteIntegrity.com

www.ingramcontent.com/pod-product-compliance
Lightning Source LLC
Chambersburg PA
CBHW060522260626

47161CB00003B/728